The Porter

Retribution in Lockdown

Rachel Parsonage

The Porter

Retribution in Lockdown

Rachel K Parsonage

First published in 2021

Edited by Alison Williams

Cover design by Carolyn Parsonage

ISBN – 978-1-914406-00-3

The Porter: Retribution in Lockdown

On the 23rd March 2020, the UK went into lockdown due to the pandemic threat of COVID-19.

After experiencing back problems, Dave Williams has exchanged working as a builder for a job as a porter in a local hospital. Dave is enjoying his job. He has lived a happy life for the past thirty years with his wife and family. His childhood, however, was not so happy.

Dave suddenly finds himself confronted with the demons of his past – he and his brother Ken were in care in the eighties, subject to a system unfit for purpose. When faced with the main perpetrator of the harm caused to them, Dave, unrecognisable in his protective equipment, finds revenge easy to execute.

Acknowledgement

To Michael Roberts of Gresford, and David Swale, teacher at Castel Alun High School in Hope - thanks for making and distributing hundreds of visors to us keyworkers and helping to keep us all safe during the COVID-19 pandemic. Thanks for looking out for us.

To Peter Jones and Fiona Knowles-Holland, thanks for casting your expert eyes over everything.

Dedications

For my dearest cousin, Harry Parsonage, the bravest guy I know.

For my selfless friend James 'Jimmy' Williams. He has never let the adversity that he has faced stop him giving up his time to help other people.

About the Author

Rachel K Parsonage works for the NHS. She lives near Wrexham in North Wales with her family. This is the second novel in the Lockdown series.

Chapters

Chapters

31st April 2020

As Dave pushed the wheelchair down the corridor, Leslie Blackwell vented steam. He complained vehemently about his leg injury, apparently sustained one evening in the park. Dave listened intently.

'I'll find out who it was who did it; they knew what they were doing alright!'

The best thing about wearing a mask was that it rendered Dave unrecognisable. In fact, it was just about the only advantage of the whole COVID-19 situation that he could think of. Blackwell couldn't see how much Dave was grinning behind his mask. Had this been a few months ago, there was every possibility that Blackwell would have recognised him. Dave pretended to listen sympathetically to his tale of woe.

'They say I'll never walk properly again. They got me in me good leg! Didn't even rob me or nothing! Almost like they did it on purpose!'

'Oh dear!'

Never walk properly again? What a terrible shame! How would he be able to go about his wretched business now? Doing his best to try and compose himself, Dave began to ask about the dreadful details of the deliberate attack on Lesley Blackwell's left shin.

'So how long was it 'til you were found then, mate?'

'Nearly two bloody hours! Left me just lying there!'

Dave felt the grin spread across his face again. Fearing that if he replied too soon he would laugh out loud, he took a deep breath.

'That's dire that, mate. How long have you had to stay in for now, then?'

'Two months! Nearly two months, for heaven's sake! It wouldn't heal, then I got an infection. My other legs dodgy an' all!'

Dave shoved his head into his shoulder to stifle the laughter, pausing again before he replied.

'Aw, you're joking. What happened to it?'

Blackwell was silent for a few seconds.

'Got hit in it with a metal bar, years ago, by a flamin' kid.'

Dave's laugh broke this time and he sniggered. He tried to cover it up with a cough. Even better, Blackwell began to squirm in the chair below him.

'Ere, you haven't got that bloody virus, have you?'

Dave left his head tucked into his shoulder for a few seconds longer just to ensure that the laugh remained contained.

'Na, na… hay fever, mate, get it every year.'

Dave hadn't had this much fun in weeks. He knew that he should shut up now, but he just couldn't help himself.

'So where did you used to work then, mate?'

Blackwell paused.

'In a kids' home.'

'So do you still work there now?'

'No.'

'So what…'

'What is this? The bloody Spanish inquisition?'

'Na, mate, just, well, making conversation seeing as you seem so keen to tell me all about what happened,' Dave managed to say, as politely as he possibly could, all the time resisting the urge to laugh.

Leslie Blackwell was evidently reticent when it came to talking about his past and Dave knew exactly why. He looked down at the man's greasy, slimy hair and wondered when he'd washed it last. He had been disgusting back then, and he was equally as disgusting now! As they neared the ward, evil thoughts began to flow through Dave's mind as he contemplated how much pain he could cause Blackwell just using the aids lying around and about in the hospital. The cast on his left leg was poking out to the side of the wheelchair. There was a large fire extinguisher situated by the door. Oh dear, he had accidentally swerved to the left …

'Pull your leg in, mate.' Unfortunately it would appear that Dave had suggested this too late.

'Aaargh!' Blackwell screamed in agony as his leg got caught between the door and the fire extinguisher.

November 1977

Manchester

It had been cold all day. Ice had formed on the inside of the single-glazed bedroom window. Dave hadn't been able to get warm since he'd come home from school. The tatty grey coat that he'd had since he was four years old had been lost. It was the coat that the other kids in school laughed at because now, two years later, the sleeves crept half way up his arms. He hadn't seen it since they'd moved to the new estate. Initially Dave had been glad that his coat had been lost. But now, as he sat and shuddered, he wished he could find it again. He didn't have many other clothes. Even though they'd moved over a month ago, his mum still hadn't unpacked most of his things.

Dave missed the old house where he had lived before with his nan. It was an old red-brick terrace in the middle of town. It had a no central heating, just a real fire in the front room. But it was always warm. It felt nice there and he knew where all his things were. He felt safe when he stayed there. His nan always washed the bedding on the double bed that he and his brother Ken shared in her spare room and it smelled lovely; not like this tatty, stained thing with no cover. Dave hadn't seen his nan for a while. His mum was supposed to have collected his things for him, but she hadn't. Every time his mum and his nan saw each other, they started arguing. His mum had told his nan not to come round anymore. Dave felt sad – he missed her and wished that he still lived with her.

At first, when his mum told them that they were moving to the new estate, they'd been excited. She said that the new house would be modern and warm. But when they arrived, he didn't like it; it was the same as the next house, and the one after that, and the one after that, as far as the eye could see for miles around. Boring realms of identical, grey, cardboard-coloured houses, with flats that towered high above. There were no nice gardens, flowers, character, familiarity; Dave didn't know anybody who lived there. Instead of the coal fires that they were used to, there were radiators on the walls to make them warm. Dave once asked his mum if she could put them on. He felt a short, sharp clip around his ear.

'Shut up about moaning about being cold; blame your dad – he's the one that walked out on us,' she replied as she swigged her glass of wine.

After that, Dave hadn't dared to complain about the fact that she hadn't made him any tea and that he was hungry. His mum was a very frightening person when she was mad. He wondered how it was that she could afford to buy wine but she didn't have any money for the radiators and the cupboards were bare of food.

He hadn't seen his dad for a long time. When he asked his mum where he had gone, she told him to shut up. Strangely enough, today his dad had turned up at the house, acting as if he had never been away. Dave and Ken had been happy to see him. Their mum hadn't been. Even though it was still early, they had been sent to bed. Raised voices emanated through the thin floors and walls from downstairs. Dave snuggled onto the mattress on the floor that he shared with Ken and put his hands over his ears. They pulled the thin, stained and tattered duvet over their heads. Still cold, he felt safe next to his big brother.

Dave was frightened. Something bad always happened after his mum and dad argued. Tonight, his tummy hurt. His mum had only made them a slice of jam on toast for tea; she said she didn't have any more food. In the school canteen, he had got into trouble for taking an extra bread roll. He knew that he shouldn't have done it, but he was so hungry that he couldn't help it. The dinner lady had seen him and he had been sent to see the headmaster. When he told him that he was hungry because he hadn't had any breakfast that morning, or tea the night before, the headmaster stopped shouting and brought him some more bread rolls from the canteen with jam and butter. He had written a letter for Dave to give to his mum when he got home. But when he gave it to her, she got really angry.

'What the hell are you doing, telling people what goes on at home? It's private, understand?'

'But Mum, you said we had to tell the truth?'

She had grabbed him by the hair and smacked him with 'the belt' across his backside. The pain made his eyes fill up as she dragged him across her bony lap. Through tears, he did what he frequently did when she got the belt out – focussed on the patterns on the utilitarian floor tiles, counting how many specks of dirt there were, and which ones were broken. The dust and cigarette ash was inches from his nose, her breath reeked of cleaning products, except nothing in this house was clean.

Dave braced himself as he heard the swish of the belt hurtling towards his back. The cracking noise echoed through the air as it made the impact with his skin. Tears dripped onto the floor. Why was she so angry? It was true, he hadn't had any tea the night before, or any breakfast in the morning! His throat choked up as he reflected on it all, how was he naughty for telling the truth? At that moment, his dad had walked back into the house.

'Now get to bed!' she'd screamed. Dave and Ken were more than happy to oblige.

Dave tried to understand why she had just hit him with the belt but he couldn't. She always told him not to lie, so he hadn't, and now that he had he was in trouble. Dave and Ken could hear raised voices.

'Think you can just turn up here, fresh out of the nick, and think everything's OK?'

'Shut up, you stupid cow. Look at the state of you. They said you'd sunk low; have you bin knocking off other blokes behind my back?'

'What if I have, you useless sod? How else do you think I pay the rent?'

'Well, you've got enough to buy booze with...'

'Yeah? You wouldn't know, doing time in the nick…'

'And why was that? Because you were spending everything on booze then; why do you think I had to rob the garage?'

'Robbed the garage? You couldn't rob fresh air! You said that was meant to set us up for life!'

'Why, you ungrateful…'

Dave pulled the damp threadbare duvet that smelled of mildew over his head. Maybe he wouldn't hear anything, maybe it would all just stop and go away. But suddenly, a piercing scream rang through the house, followed by the thud of the front door. He heard Ken gasp and felt his body go rigid. Dave began to whimper, dread curdling in his stomach. Neither boy dared move for some time, their limbs growing stiff in the cold. Eventually Ken dared to poke his head out. It was all very strange.

There had been a lot of noise, now it had just stopped and everything was deathly silent.

'Shall we go downstairs?' whispered Dave.

'Dunno! Do you remember what happened last time? When we heard a man here and I went downstairs she thumped my head so hard I got a black eye.'

'Which man? She always has men here.'

'The one last week that was really old.'

'Oh yeah, I remember now, that one!'

They waited a bit longer.

'Maybe she's just gone to sleep? Like she does when she drinks wine?'

'Dunno, she sounded like she was really hurt,' said Ken. He got out of the bed and crept downstairs. Dave dared not move. What if she got the belt out again? He was still in pain from the beating that he'd had this evening.

'No, Ken, don't go.'

'I'll be OK, I'll be quiet, don't worry!' he whispered.

Dave stopped breathing while he listened for the creaking of the stairs, fearing that if his mum heard Ken she would shoot up in a fearsome rage. But Ken didn't come back. Dave began to worry; where was he? What if his mum had seen Ken? What if he had got into serious trouble? What if she had taken him outside or somewhere to give him a hiding? Dave remained silent. Slowly, shattered, he drifted off into sleep.

He hadn't been asleep for long when he was woken up by a friendly policeman, who wrapped him in a big warm blanket and carried him into a car. Dave smiled to himself as the warmth enveloped his body. The policeman took him and Ken to the station and gave them some toast and a big drink of milk. They devoured the food and the policeman watched them with a strange look of contented sympathy.

'Where's my mum?' asked Dave. 'Why have we come here?'

Ken started crying and buried his head in his hands.

'Ken, what's the matter? Why are you crying?'

'Just shut up, Dave.' Ken looked angry and upset. The tears continued to roll down his face. Dave didn't understand what was going on, or why Ken was so mad at him for asking; he just wanted to know where his mum was.

'Hey, come on, lads,' said the friendly policeman. 'You had enough toast? What about some biscuits? I think I might have some digestives in the cupboard.'

****

After that, they were sent to a house to live with a nice lady and man. They had lots of nice food, and Dave had a nice warm bed, showers and nice clothes. They bought him a nice warm grey parka coat with a furry hood that fitted him. When Dave asked Ken where his mum and dad were, he told him to shut up. Ken pretended otherwise, but he always looked as if he was going to cry. Dave couldn't make head nor tail of what was going on, but he felt happy living somewhere without his mum. He didn't want to go back and live with her.

'Ken, do you think we'll have to go back to live at Mums?'

'No,' said Ken, sharply.

Ken was right, they never saw their mum again.

A few weeks later, life got even better. Dave and Ken were sent to live back at their nan's house. It was lovely, warm and clean, with the aroma of coal fires and rolled up tobacco. Nan was firm but fair. The eight years that Dave spent living with his nan were the happiest of his childhood. It always felt nice to be with her. He stopped worrying about what he was saying or doing and forgot how scared he was of being himself. She made toast with homemade jam and lots of butter with scones and lovely big roast dinners. She took them to football and scouts. Every year they went on holiday to Rhyl in a caravan. Never scolding them unless absolutely necessary, she taught them manners and respect.

But one day when Dave returned from school there was an ambulance parked outside. His nan was being carried outside on a stretcher. Her lips were blue. Her wispy, fluffy, grey hair was drenched in sweat that made it stick to her forehead. Her usually rosy cheeks with the lines like soft crepe paper were grey, just like the rest of her face.

'Nan!' he shouted, running up to her.

She turned her head slowly to the side.

'I'm not well, love,' she whispered

'Nan, I love you, Nan, where are you going? Please, Nan, don't you leave us as well!'

'Promise me something, you'll be a good lad? You'll stay out of trouble? And away from crime? And drugs? For me. I love you so much!' she said as she grabbed Dave's hand tightly and kissed it. 'I'd never leave you, Dave, I love you, I'll be here,' she pointed to his heart, 'always.'

'Sorry, son, we'll have to take her now,' said the ambulance man as he pulled the stretcher into the back of the ambulance. 'She's really not well! She's been having chest pain that won't stop with her spray.'

Ken appeared round the corner.

'Nan!' he shouted as he ran to the back of the ambulance. 'What's the matter?'

'She's not well, son,' said the ambulance man. 'We need to take her to hospital quickly. Go home, lads.'

'But this is our home. We live with our nan,' said Dave.

'Where's your mum and dad? Have you got a phone number for them or anything?'

Dave and Ken looked at each other.

'Er, no,' said Ken.

'Aw, don't they have a phone?' asked the ambulance man.

There was silence for some time, until Ken spoke.

'No. Our mum's dead, and my dad's in prison for killing her.'

So matter-of-fact. Dave stared up at him in shock; Ken raised his eyebrows knowingly. Nobody had ever told Dave what had happened to his mum, or where his dad had gone. Every time he asked his nan, she didn't reply. Ken wouldn't talk about it. Now it all made sense! The ambulance man stared at them with sadness and pity.

'Jump in and say goodbye to her quick, then we'll have to take her.'

Dave and Ken climbed into the back of the ambulance and hugged their nan.

'Nan, please get better, please don't leave us like everyone else does.'

'I love you, Nan, you're not just our nan, you're our mum.'

They both began to sob. She gripped them with her pudgy hands. They were usually warm, and comfortable, and soft. Now they were cold, but, strangely, sweaty.

'Be good lads for me, I love you both,' she whispered. Her words seemed to be becoming weaker with every second that passed.

'Don't worry, we'll get you sorted, lads,' said the ambulance man who was in the back with her.

Nan had a bad heart and had had a heart attack the previous year. She hadn't been able to do as much since and often had to use her spray that stopped her having pain in her chest. But today, the ambulance men said that it had stopped working. Now she looked terrible. What if she died? Fear shot up into Dave's throat; it was all that he could do to stop himself vomiting over the pavement.

'Not her too, Ken; she can't leave us.'

'I know.' Ken seemed dazed.

'She'll get better, won't she?'

'Yeah, she's in the ambulance and she's going to hospital, they'll make her better… won't they?'

They stood and watched the ambulance as it drove down the road with the blue lights flashing and the siren switched on.

'Why didn't you tell me? About Mum?'

'Dunno,' said Ken. 'But it was that horrible, I never wanted you to even have to imagine it.'

They watched the ambulance turn the corner and disappear onto the main road which led to the hospital. They never saw their nan again.

October 1987

Dave sat in the car – off again. He was sick of this! Ever since Nan had died, he had been moved around different houses to live with different foster carers every few months. He had to keep moving his stuff (not that he had much) and getting used to new people, sometimes new schools, new routines - why he couldn't just be left in one place was beyond him! Last year, he had been split up from Ken; apparently they were just too much of a handful together. The man and lady that they had lived with - the ones that had made them pray before eating and go to church - had said that they couldn't cope with the boys' bad behaviour. They had been told off in school for fighting and then they had been caught smoking. Dave knew kids who did far worse things than him and Ken and no one sent them to live elsewhere! Not that Dave minded, he hadn't liked living there anyway.

Ken had been sent to a children's home in North Wales, but he had started sniffing glue and taking drugs. When he was sixteen, he had moved into his own flat. Dave wasn't allowed to see him anymore. Now Dave was going to a children's home in the town in North Wales where Ken lived. He only had a month until he was sixteen, when, if he wanted to, he could leave the care system – something that he fully intended to do.

He'd heard bad things about the home from other kids. They told stories about staff abusing them, making them do bad things for sweets and toys, beating them up and so on. He hadn't seen Ken to ask if it was true; it all sounded a bit far-fetched. Surely those things couldn't happen in this day and age? You got sent to a kids' home if your parents died, or if they were crap or cruel to you, or bad people. They were supposed to be places that kids could have a better life, weren't they? And if it was true, why hadn't those homes been shut down? Why was he being sent there now?

The big house loomed up in front of him as they approached. On the outside, it looked like the set of a TV series from olden times. Dave couldn't fathom why he felt so uneasy. Even though it was old, it didn't seem as if a ghost was going to jump out from behind the trees, or a vampire was going to open the large oak door, or as if there were dead bodies buried in the garden; it was a different kind of creepy. Dave tried to reason with himself that it was simply because of all the stories that he'd been told.

He walked with his social worker through the old stone entrance into the hallway and down the corridors. As the large oak front door shut loudly behind them, chills spilled down Dave's spine and his heart began to beat faster – that always happened when he was worried.

'Look, don't be scared, I'll come back and visit you the week after next to see how you're getting on,' she said, sensing his apprehension.

'I don't want to stay here. I wish I could be with Ken.'

'I know.' She sighed. 'But Ken can't look after you, Dave. He's not capable at the moment. Look, it's only for a few weeks…'

Dave nodded. He already knew they'd never let him live with Ken – not after what he'd been doing! But Dave would be sixteen soon – then they couldn't stop him!

The house looked from the outside as if it should look posh on the inside, but it wasn't; the ceilings had been lowered, making the corridors seem oppressive, the once grand entrance and rooms appeared to have been made smaller – clinical and devoid of any soul, as if every inch of space had been accounted for to ensure that it was put to maximum use, to the cost of the once aesthetically pleasing purpose for which the building had been designed. The whole building felt as if it was closing in on him. Behind the façade of modernisation and improvements to be "fit for purpose", the freshly painted walls were trying to whisper something to him, but what?

Eventually after they had walked down the rabbit warren of corridors, his social worker knocked on the door of an office.

'Well, hello,' said the man who opened the door. He was middle-aged, balding, overweight, yet dressed in a smart grey suit and tie. Whoever he was, he seemed familiar with Dave's social worker, Penny.

'Hi, Reg. This is Dave.'

Dave's social worker rattled off the usual dialogue; who Dave was, his hobbies and interests, where he had lived before, and so on. Reg listened intently, then started to ask Dave about his family. To focus on this seemed unusual. Two minutes in and Dave had only told him about his family situation. Reg asked no further questions. Why wasn't he focussing on what Dave liked to do? Or on his achievements? Like when he won "player of the season" in football last year?

'Don't worry, we're your family now,' said Reg, with a grin.

Dave couldn't shake off the unnerving feeling that was enveloping him. He didn't want Reg to be his family. Over the years, he had found it increasingly difficult to trust anyone or what they said. When he could trust someone, he usually got a vibe from them, like the kind of vibe that he had always got from his nan or his social worker. Dave wasn't getting that vibe from Reg. The man's demeanour was not quite genuine enough to believe and he couldn't look Dave straight in the eye.

'OK, then, Dave, I'll see you in a week or two,' said Penny. 'In the meantime, I'll leave you in the capable hands of Mr. Evans, or Reg as you can call him.' She smiled as she left. She was going, leaving him here, in this overwhelmingly large house, with Reg? Dave tried to return a diminishing smile. He didn't want her to leave him, not here, with Reg. His heart began to pound and his throat went dry. All the time, Reg stood there with an odd half-smile on his face; the kind of smile that someone had to force; the kind of smile that didn't come naturally.

'Look,' she said, sensing his unease and putting her hand on his shoulder, 'it's OK to be scared, it's normal. But you'll be alright. And if you're not, you can tell me all about it next time I see you.'

Reg saw the social worker out of the office. As he returned, Dave looked up at him. The man's eyes looked deeply into his and the smile slid from his face. He grabbed Dave by the ear and pinned his head on the desk.

'You listen here, and you listen good…any messing around from you, and you'll have the thick end of my belt, you got that? You do exactly what we tell you here.'

'Y… y… yes,' whispered Dave. He felt his ear press against the desk and fill up with blood. The longer that it stayed pressed there, the longer it felt as if it was about to be ripped off. Reg grabbed Dave's head, pulled it up and slammed it down on the desk.

'I couldn't quite hear you. What did you say?'

'I said y…yes.'

'Yes who?' asked Reg. 'What's my name?'

'Er, Mr… Mr… Evans?'

'Sir, it's sir! From now on, you do as you're told. Any dicking around, not listening to staff, if I even see you in my office, you will be very sorry!' he said, indicating to the belt that was tied around his waist. 'Is that clear?'

Dave nodded.

'What did you say?'

'I said, yes.'

The man grabbed his head again.

'Yes who?'

'Yes, sir,' replied Dave as Evans pulled his head up. He shut his eyes as he did so. This could not be happening. Maybe he was in a nightmare. A terrible nightmare. If he shut his eyes, maybe it would all stop.

'And who knows, we might even become friends, mightn't we?' Evans said with a sneer, brushing a hand down Dave's top. It wasn't as if there was any dirt on Dave's top - there was no need for Reg to touch him there or anywhere else for that matter. Dave felt his heart begin to pound faster as the man's hand brushed against him. His warm forehead felt as if it would explode as an impending sense of doom and hopelessness washed over him. He felt moisture on his lips; it tasted of salt. By now, his heart was pounding so hard that he could feel the veins in his neck pulsating.

A horrible thought began to cross Dave's mind as the stark realisation about what he had been told by the other children began to sink in – what if it was all true? The overwhelming terror that had consumed him made Dave's mouth dry. Dave had met lots of people that he didn't like in his time, but Evans was something else, on an entirely different level. Cold and calculating. He had acted up for the social worker, and then the minute she had gone, he had changed. It was all pre-meditated: what was he going to do to him next? Dave wanted to get out of there, to go home. But then he realised – he had no home, this place was home!

There was a knock at the door. Another man entered – he was thin with lanky brown hair and an unshaven face, cold, narrowed eyes and a furrowed brow. Younger than Evans, he smelled strange, of mild, pungent sweat and cigarette smoke mixed with cheap aftershave. Dave had smelled that smell before – Lambert and Butler, the same cheap cigarettes that Ken had robbed from the shop when they had got into trouble at their last placement.

'Aah, here's Mr, Blackwell. I don't believe you've met him, have you? Leslie, this is young Dave. Mum died when he was little, his nan very sadly passed away, no contact with his dad who's in prison for killing his mum, no other family! Just Ken, you know Ken, from our other establishment, no longer there? Just sniffing glue in the flat now?'

A creepy smile spread across Blackwell's face and he and Evans smirked at each other. Why was he telling this other creepy-looking man that they'd all died? What did he mean about Ken?

The ceilings seemed to be dropping further and the floor moving up simultaneously. The scant winter light coming in from the window was almost blinding. Petrified, Dave wracked his brains for ways to get out of there. He looked around the room in desperation. There was only the window looking out onto the drive. It was shut and he had no idea how to open it. He scoured the room in desperation to find something, anything that he could use to smash the old single glass pane of the huge sash window – nothing. For a few seconds, Dave contemplated smashing through the window, but the drop to the ground below was a long way. If he bolted now, maybe he could catch up with his social worker? As he looked, he saw that she was just getting back into her car. He turned his attention to the door. The creepy younger man was standing in front of it – Dave was trapped.

'Yeah, we know Ken, he was a good friend of ours, wasn't he, Mr. Evans?' said Mr. Blackwell, flashing his brown teeth at Dave.

Dave knew that Blackwell was lying. Dave did not doubt for one second that Ken would have despised Blackwell and Evans just as much as he did. But what did

Blackwell mean? Had he or Evans pinned Ken's ear to the table as a welcome when they got there? Had they brushed him down with their hands and made him uncomfortable? Scared the life out of him by doing something else? What had they done to Ken? Was it something terrible? Was that why he had gone off the rails? Started sniffing glue and taking drugs? Dave could taste the sweat dripping down his forehead onto his lips.

'Yes, so, welcome to the home. I hope you'll remember our little chat, and remember that you need to stay out of trouble. You scratch our backs, and we'll scratch yours,' said Evans. 'You've only got a few weeks with us until you're sixteen; only a few weeks, Mr. Blackwell. I think we've got just enough time to get to know young Dave here, haven't we?'

Blackwell smirked.

'Isn't that right, David?'

'Y…y… yes s… sir.' Dave managed to reply, unable to find a single drop of saliva with which to lubricate his tongue.

Evans flashed him another creepy grin.

'Leslie, will you please take this young man to his room?'

Blackwell indicated for Dave to go with him. Dave had never felt as glad to get out of somewhere in his life. Terrified, he began to wonder where Blackwell was taking him next, and what he was going to do with him.

He was escorted down an endless rabbit warren of corridors. They reached the dormitories and Blackwell shoved him through a door.

'Unpack your stuff. I'll be back in five minutes. And if you're still unpacking, anything left is getting burned. Yeah?'

Dave nodded his head.

Dave wanted to leave everything where it was in his bag and get out of there. Maybe he could run away? But where could he go? What if they brought him back? They would be mad with him. In a state of disbelief and bewilderment, Dave quickly unpacked. If he got his head down and did what he was told, maybe he would get on here? Maybe they would leave him alone? Intuition was telling him that it wasn't going to be that easy, and to take the next chance that he could to get as far away from there as he could.

Dave had put his important things in a plastic wallet in his bag – the pictures that he had of his nan, some of him and Ken, his certificates and his football medal. He folded the wallet as tightly as he could without damaging any of them and put it in the large pocket in the back of his jeans. Shortly after, Blackwell returned.

'You done?'

Dave nodded.

'Right, come with me.'

Blackwell led him into the gardens outside. There were several other boys there digging flower beds and weeding. They stopped and stared at Dave.

'New kid, look.'

'You're getting it.'

'Yeah, whatever,' replied Dave defiantly; inside he was terrified.

One of the boys in the group looked over at Blackwell who nodded at him, then he walked over to Dave.

'Oh yeah? Think you're hard, do you?'

Dave looked over at Blackwell to see if he was going to intervene. Given that he was a member of staff, perhaps he would try and calm the situation down. But Blackwell just sparked up a cigarette, watching them out of his cold, narrow eyes. The boy walked up to Dave and smacked his fist straight into the side of his head. Stars flashed before Dave's eyes as he fell to the floor. He covered his head with his arms as kicks rained into his chest from the boy's trainers. He looked up in desperation for someone to help him; nobody was there, nobody except for Blackwell who he could just about make out, still sitting there, puffing on his cigarette. There was a metal spade next to him on the ground. Dave grabbed it and swung it into the boy's leg. The boy yelped in pain and bent double as Dave got up and kicked him hard in the stomach, sending him flying across the grass into a flowerbed.

'Yeah, alright, that's enough,' said Blackwell.

They had just had a scrap in full view of Blackwell and everyone else... it had lasted for some time. Why had Blackwell not intervened sooner? Was he not supposed to be supervising them? Making sure that they all kept in line? Dave got the distinct impression that he had only eventually said anything because Dave was getting the better of the other boy.

'You're all supposed to be digging here, now get digging!' Blackwell said angrily.

Gradually, the group dispersed and everyone picked up a spade. As they began digging, Dave made sure that he kept as far away from the other boy as possible so as not to antagonise him and make the situation worse. As he worked away, he kept one eye on the boy and one on the other members of the group. Dave hated this place. Why was Blackwell not looking after them like he was supposed to? Why did he work there if he didn't like kids? Was he just evil? Or sick in the head?

That evening, tea was served in a large dining room. Dave took his tray, got his dinner and sat down at a table alone. He didn't feel like eating. He worried about what was going to happen next and his stomach started cramping. He tried to eat. The sausage roll and frozen sweetcorn and peas weren't particularly appetising. In his mind, he went over the stories that other boys had told him about care homes. Dave's heart sank as the realisation previously only suspected was now becoming obvious – maybe the kids that had lived in care homes had been right all along? Even though he had never said anything, maybe Ken had hated it too? Maybe he should have listened? And if that was the case, what were Blackwell and Evans planning to do to him?

After tea, he was allowed to go to the room that he shared with four other boys. One of them was the boy that he had had the altercation with outside.

'Alright?' Dave muttered to him. Maybe if he showed him that he was OK and that there were no hard feelings, he would leave him alone.

'Piss off!'

Dave shrugged and lay down on his bed, picking up a magazine.

'You're gonna be very sorry about before!' the boy said.

'Look, mate, I don't want no trouble. You started on me, keep your hands to yourself and we'll be OK.'

The boy spat something gruffly at Dave and walked out of the room.

'Mate,' said the boy lying on the next bed. He spoke softly. 'You need to watch your back with Dennis... he's one of Blackwell's favourites'.

'Yeah, thanks.'

'No, seriously, I saw you today, leathering him in the garden. He's one of Blackwell's favourites...he will have you for that! Just get your head down, say nothing.'

'So what's the score? Do you just let people kick you in up here?'

The boy shrugged his shoulders. 'Well, yeah. Blackwell is pure evil, trust me, fighting back is not worth the hassle.'

'I hate it here already; I ain't staying. I'm phoning my social worker tomorrow'.

The other boy laughed. 'Mate, we've all tried that. There's nowhere else to go. If they think you've told anyone, your life will be even worse than it is now. Plus, next place is Young Offenders. Meant to be worse than here! You don't want to go there!'

Dave had heard about borstal, which was now renamed and rebranded as "Young Offenders". He'd met a few lads during his time in care who had been there. They said that it was hard, but it was OK. They certainly didn't seem messed up by it, or speak about it reluctantly as they did about the care homes.

'So who told you that?' asked Dave.

'Blackwell and Evans, they said that whatever they do to you here, they'll do it twenty times worse to you in borstal, and you won't come back out alive!'

'Mate, I've met a few guys from borstal. They say it's not that bad. Sounds to me like they're making it sound worse than it is. But thanks for the advice.'

'Seriously, keep your head down. Lads have gone missing from here; they said they've run away, we've never seen them again. I've seen it! Slit wrists, attempted hangings. Please don't tell them I told you!' As he spoke, the other boy's eyes were wide. Dave could tell that even though he appeared to be accustomed to the situation, he was clearly scared stiff of Blackwell and Evans. Dave felt palpitations beginning to build up in his chest again.

'Haven't you got anyone who can get you out?'

The boy shook his head again, his face melancholy. 'No, it's just me left... they know that. I've got nobody to complain to; they know they can do whatever they want to me and I can't tell anyone.'

The boy's evident acquiescence to this horrific situation was beginning to freak Dave out. He had to get out! Anywhere had to be better than this! Even young offenders!

'So what's your name, mate?'

'Matthew.'

'How long you been here for?'

'I've been here since I was eleven, when my mum and dad died.'

'Sorry to hear that. What's it like?'

Matthew didn't reply for some time.

'It's bad.'

'Well, can't you just... leave? Or ask to be sent somewhere else?'

Matthew shook his head. 'Tried that, they just send you back. I tried to tell my social worker. He had a word with them, then I just got a beating and for a bit it was even worse than it was before.'

That first night, as Dave lay in bed, silent tears dripped down his face. He had never felt so alone. He had no one, no one that he could turn to, no one he could trust, no one to look out for him. The figures of authority, supposed to be looking after him, were doing anything but. For the first time ever, Dave even began to wonder if it would actually be better to go back and try and live with his murderous Dad. He was trapped! Every time he had someone that he loved, and trusted, his nan, Ken, they were taken away from him. Now, here he was, at the cruel mercy of the authorities where all the bad things that anyone had ever told him about were turning out to be true. Who would ever believe him if he told anyone? He was just some kid with a grudge against the staff from a care home. Surely kids had complained before? It just wasn't fair! Why couldn't he be back with his nan again, where he was happy?

The last time that Dave had seen Ken, he'd been off his face. Dave knew Ken had started smoking pot, sniffing glue, and had stopped going to school. The worst part of it all was that Dave was beginning to see why he did it – it was so he could forget; to forget seeing their mum dead, and losing their nan, to forget about the foster homes, the time in care, the terrible life that they'd had – but most of all to forget about this. If the home up the road that Ken had been in was anything like this one, Dave knew exactly why he had started taking drugs! How Dave wished that Ken had been there when his nan asked him to promise to keep on the straight and narrow; she would have known what to do. Her words rang in his ears.

Over the next few days, Dave heard more things from some of the other lads that made his heart freeze, some genuine slips of the tongue, some more contrived. It seemed to be well known that Reg the 'Boss Man' Evans and Leslie Blackwell were very fond of young boys, especially those with no family, no one that they could complain to. Dave realised that he fitted into this category: perfect fodder for the Boss Man, Blackwell and whoever else he was yet to meet with the same evil intentions. He shuddered as he heard the conversations going on in and around the home between the other boys.

'Where did you get the new bike?'

'Boss man Reg.'

'Ah so you're the new favourite he takes to his room every night?'

'What happened to your eye?'

'Blackwell smacked me when I tried to get away.'

'What did you bother doing that for? There's nowhere to go.'

'Couldn't stand it any longer.'

Forget it, mate, you've got no family, no one's going to look out for you.'

Dave was alone – Blackwell and Evans knew that. He was just some kid, who was dispensable, expendable, someone that no one would bother about if he just "went missing". No one except his junkie brother! He kept replaying the conversation in the office that he had had with Evans and Blackwell when he first arrived.

'You've only got a few weeks here until you're sixteen...'

He didn't have long.

Over the next few days, Dave was given more advice from Matthew; advice that he didn't feel like taking.

'If Blackwell asks you to go in the shower with him, just go.'

'If they come into the room in the night and wake you up, pretend you've got a bad cough.'

'Even if you've got no family, pretend you've got some long lost relative who occasionally gets in touch.'

Every day, in the garden, in the classroom, in the dinner hall, in the dormitories, kids were half-killing each other. Some workers did their best and seemed OK, but those like Blackwell just sat there, making it worse, stirring things up. Some lads - the favourites - who didn't appear to be doing much at all, got privileges, leaving the others who worked hard with nothing.

A few nights later, just after lights out, Dave was lying in bed awake, thinking about everything. It always took him a long time to get to sleep. He heard the floorboards in the corridor creaking, and the door opened. He could just about make out Blackwell's face in the light as he came into the room.

'You, come on,' he said to Dennis. 'Now, we haven't got all night. If you want that remote-controlled car for Christmas, you're gonna have to earn it.'

Dave pretended to be asleep, watching through half-open eyes as Blackwell dragged a half-asleep Dennis up out of bed and marched him down the corridor. There was no protesting, nobody else stirred, nobody else said anything. Dave wasn't stupid; there was only one reason a grown man would wake up a young lad and order him to go somewhere with him. Dave was petrified and couldn't sleep. A short while later, Dennis returned. Dave could hear his muffled sobs in the bunk underneath him. Dave realised that if he didn't get out of there, he would end up being one of the ones called out of bed to join Evans and Blackwell in the office in the middle of the night.

The next evening when Dave went for his shower, he heard a voice in the next cubicle where one of the other boys, Marlon, was washing.

'Get yourself stripped off and get in the shower.'

It was Blackwell's voice. Marlon began to cough.

'You had a cough last week, surely it's gone by now?'

'No, it's still bad.'

'Well, I don't want your filthy cough.'

Dave stood in the shower; his heart stopped beating. There were three shower cubicles, all were in use. What if Blackwell came for him next? He heard Blackwell move to what sounded like the one to left of Marlon. When Dave got out of the shower, Blackwell was standing there, just watching the boy who had showered on the other side of Dave getting dressed.

Dave avoided the other lads. He felt that if he spent time with them he would be drawn into something, into an arguments, or a fight, to a point that the culture of this place would start to become his normal. Dave was determined that wasn't going to happen. Besides, he didn't trust anyone. Every lunchtime during his free time, he walked alone in the grounds, acting like a loner, but secretly scouring the place for an escape route. Every time he saw Blackwell or Evans, his heart skipped a beat as he wondered when he would get the call to go with one of them into the office or the showers.

Marlon's fake cough and Matthew's advice had given him an idea. After free time, they were all ordered to work in the garden. The next day, Dave scoured the ground for some uncut grass, the long type that gathers around tree stumps. Dave was allergic to grass and suffered from severe hay fever. It made his nose run and gave him a tight chest. He picked the grass and rubbed the stems over his face and up his nose. He rubbed at his eyes as he felt them starting to stream, as mucus began to accumulate in his nose and run down the back of his throat. His throat tightened and his lips began to tingle.

'You…' said Blackwell, ordering one of the younger boys to follow him into the shed. Dave noticed the look of fear on the boy's face as he put his spade down and began to follow Blackwell obediently. A short while later, the boy emerged with a thick lip, looking ashamed. He hung his head down low as he walked back out, picked his spade up and carried on digging. Nobody spoke to him; everybody knew where he had been and what had happened. Blackwell wasn't far behind him, walking straight in Dave's direction. With his eyes already swollen, Dave pulled some remnants of grass from out of his pocket and rubbed them over his nose.

He sneezed.

'Urgh!' Blackwell looked at Dave's swollen, bloodshot eyes and the dried mucus marks running down his nose. 'Keep away from me with your germs.'

'Yes, sir.' That was exactly what he intended to do, at least until he could find a more permanent solution to his predicament. Dave knew that he couldn't do this forever, and that, before long, Blackwell would become suspicious.

Dave began to make a plan to escape, where he could stay out of the home for the next few weeks, lie low and not come back. He needed to wait for just a couple more days when he got his pocket money allowance. But later that day, while looking for some long grass in a disused area where someone had chopped some of the trees down, Dave found exactly what he needed just in case he got into trouble before this. A plan began to form in his head.

The next day, Blackwell was back on shift. They had been ordered to sweep the leaves from the driveway at the front of the house. Dave had not yet had chance to collect any grass, but just in case, concealed in his coat was his new find. He had hoped for just another day or two, but that wasn't going to happen.

'You, come and help me,' Blackwell said to Dave, beckoning him to follow him into the shed where the garden tools were kept.

Dave took a deep breath. This was it – his time had come. He picked up his coat from off the floor where he had strategically placed the item and followed Blackwell to the shed, folding his arms as he walked, secretly clutching his find into his chest. He knew exactly why Blackwell wanted him to go in there with him, and he was ready.

'You won't need your coat where we're going,' said Blackwell with an evil smirk.

Keeping a safe distance behind Blackwell as he walked into the shed, Dave pulled his coat off as he entered. He placed it on the floor just inside the door. Once inside, Blackwell walked up to Dave, grabbed his head and shoved it into the radiator. Dave felt a large lump beginning to form on his forehead. The room span around him and stars zipped in front of his eyes. He could just about make out Evans standing in front of him. Dave's heart sank; he hadn't realised that there would be two of them – he needed to think fast.

'Get up!' Blackwell ordered as he slammed Dave's head into the radiator again. Dave had expected this and put his arms out as he did so. The contact between his head and the radiator was minimal.

'Aaargh.' He screamed, holding his head, pretending to be in more pain than he was. 'My head.'

'Now, Mr, Evans here, he wants you to be nice to him. Shut up, do what we say, and it won't take long.'

Dave stayed on the floor, moving backwards slowly, feigning disorientation and clutching his head in his hands, all the time moving stealthily backwards in order to position himself near his coat - only a few more inches to go.

'Aw, come over here, sweetie, come to Uncle Reg,' said Evans, walking towards Dave. Blackwell went to grab him again,

'Come on then, let's be having you,' said Evans as he began to take off his belt.

Dave knew exactly what it was that he was going to do to him; he wasn't coming anywhere near him. As Blackwell neared, Dave pulled out the axe that he had hidden under his coat and swung it as hard as he could into the man's right shin. Blackwell let out a blood-curdling scream.

'Aaargh!' he yelled. 'You little…' Hopping around in agonising pain, he eventually collapsed on the floor in front of Dave.

Dave stood up. 'I can't hear you, what did you say?' he asked Blackwell, raising the axe above his head.

'N… n… n… nothing! Just leave me, please…' said Blackwell, a whimpering mess on the floor.

All the time, keeping one eye on Evans, Dave watched as Blackwell's pupils constricted in shock and the colour drained from his face. Dave started laughing, slowly at first, and then more loudly. Momentarily taking his eye off Evans, Dave looked Blackwell straight in the eye as he brought the axe down again on what remained of his right shin bone. As Blackwell lay incapacitated on the floor with blood pouring from the front of his trouser leg, Dave couldn't resist going back one last time. He stamped his foot down as hard as he could on Blackwell's shin bone, feeling a sharp crack as he did so.

Blackwell let out another bloodcurdling scream. There was something cathartic about that scream; it filled Dave's heart with happiness. A smile spread across his face and he felt the part of his heart that had stopped beating since he had arrived at the place began to feel warm again.

'Aaargh, aaargh!'

Screams of agony rang through the shed. Dave looked over at Evans. He was standing with his mouth, open shaking his head from side to side, his face white.

'Now come on, d… don't be stupid, put the axe down!'

As Dave walked towards him, Evans walked backwards with his arms out, his palms facing upwards. He was not a tall man, he was of Dave's height, just well-built. Dave wasn't scared of him; he'd taken on harder.

'N… n… now, don't be stupid, put it down,' Evans whimpered. 'Y… y… you'll end up in young offenders! Is that what you want? You… you think it's bad here, it's ten times worse there! We'll make a deal, we'll leave you alone, we… we…' He put his right arm above his head to protect his face.

'This, you filthy nonce, this is for you!' hissed Dave as he swung the axe over his head once more and hacked the blade into Evans' forearm as hard as he possibly could. Evans let out an agonising scream as he staggered about, holding his arm. Dave contemplated swinging the axe into Evans' other arm, but he had just narrowly avoided the man's face, and Evans was moving about too much for Dave to get a clean shot. Instead, he swung it as hard as he could into Evans' nearest shin. He had more than put his plan into place, now he had to stop.

'Better go and phone the police then, fellas, I'm off... see you later!'

Leaving Blackwell and Evans on the floor, Dave left through the front door of the shed, doubling back around the side before anybody noticed, making his way swiftly through the back of the gardens towards the road outside. He kept his head low as he crossed the perimeter fence. The road to the side of the building led back to the town. If he sprinted through the field next to it and kept his head down behind the shrubbery, out of sight, Dave reckoned he could reach the middle of town in less than ten minutes. He dared not wander the other way into the hills just in case he got lost, or they found him. He threw the axe into a ditch filled with muddy water as he crossed over the old stone wall into the fields and ran, faster than he had in his life. He didn't stop, not even when he thought that his lungs would collapse.

After just over a mile, he'd reached the outskirts of town. Keeping his head low he morphed into the busy streets. He had no idea where he was going. All he knew was that he was getting away from there, from them. Soon, the police would be looking for him. *But now where?* He had nowhere to go, no one to turn to, and no money.

His plan was to lie low until he was caught. If he could duck and dive until his sixteenth birthday, they couldn't make him go back there. If the police caught him, they would have to send him to young offenders instead. Surely it had to be better there? Confident that he wasn't being followed, he walked towards the centre of town and darted in and out of the crowds of people.

In the centre of town, some old buildings were being demolished. Next to them, new ones were going up. Dave stood and watched, pausing to catch his breath and his thoughts. He had an idea. He went up to the gate and asked to speak to the foreman.

'Excuse me, mate, you got any jobs going?'

The foreman nodded.

'Who for pal?'

'Well... me.'

'Need a hod carrier over there, pal, usually twenty-five quid a day. It's a bit late, so call it twenty.' He indicated to a pile of bricks and a ramp. 'Start now if you like.'

Dave nodded. It was nearly ten o'clock. If he could get the rest of the day in, he could at least earn some money.

All day, Dave sweated, carrying bricks. Surely nobody would think to look for him here? On a building site? His gut wrenched every time he saw a police car drive past on the road outside. It was a cold, autumn day. But he felt grateful that he was busy, grateful that the police wouldn't come looking for him there.

'What's your name, mate?' the foreman asked at the end of the day, handing Dave his wages.

'Steve.'

'You coming back tomorrow?'

Dave nodded. 'Yep.'

'OK, eight o'clock? See you then.'

Dave turned left out of the site the way that his feet took him. Where should he go? What should he do? Maybe it would only be a matter of time before the police caught him. But now he had money. There were a few hotels in the area, offering rooms for twenty pounds a night. But he was starving and thirsty. He hadn't eaten or had a drink for hours. It was a toss-up between somewhere to stay and something to eat; Dave's stomach won. Having a bit of money meant that he didn't need to draw attention to himself, by shoplifting, or begging on the streets. Dave wandered around the side streets of town for a while with his hood up. He was freezing, ducking every time a police car went past, feeling his heart rate increase and palpitations rise up in his chest.

He went into the first shop that he came to and bought himself a large bottle of water and some crisps, chocolate and a sausage roll to eat, together with a packet of cheap cigarettes – not Lambert and Butler! Dave knew that he would never ever smoke them again. Outside, he devoured the food. When he finished, weary, he walked aimlessly around town. Soon he came to a park. He entered and sat on a bench in the middle, out of sight of the road and the streets. He stayed there for some time, drinking his water and contemplating where to go and what to do next as he smoked a cigarette – that was the nicest cigarette that he had ever smoked! As the nicotine rush hit his brain he began to think more clearly, to rationalise his thoughts.

He had heard that there was a homeless shelter in the middle of town; maybe he could go there? But that was an obvious place for them to look. Maybe he could get the train and go back to Manchester? But if he did, what would he do when he got there? He had nowhere to go and nobody to turn to. Yeah, he had aunts and uncles, but he hadn't seen them for some time. And where had they been when his mum and nan had died? It was as if when his nan died, the part of him that was his life in Manchester had died too. He felt no connection to the place. Now that the only other person that he loved had died there, it reminded him of fear, death, and misery.

At least here, he could earn some money while he made his plans. Dave didn't know anybody apart from Ken. Even though he had the address for Ken's flat in town, he dare not go there: it would be the first place that they would look.

It began to drizzle. Before long Dave was frozen. The colder he got, the more irrational his thought processes became. He began to wonder if he should do something to get himself arrested, so that he could get put in the cells for the night. At least it would be warm in there, but then if they found out who he was and where he was from, surely they would send him back. Maybe if he went to hospital and said that he had stomach cramps he could stay there for the night? But then they would want to know where his parents were, who had parental responsibility for him and where he lived. Dave was beginning to see exactly why people ran away from places like the home, and then went back. Having nowhere to go in this freezing cold weather was nearly as bad as staying in a warm building with vile people and being abused. Chain smoking his cigarettes was now failing to calm him down. He needed to go somewhere and be at least half-warm away from the rain.

Another figure sloped into the park and sat on the bench next to him, a man who also looked as if he had nowhere else to be. He pulled out a needle and rolled his sleeve up.

'S... scuse me mate, do you know if there's anywhere you can stay, if you've got nowhere to go, like?'

The man paused. Under the dim streetlight, he looked up at Dave, his skin sallow, eyes devoid of emotion set back in shrunken hollows; it was the face of someone who had had the last remains of life or hope cruelly removed long ago. He looked old, too old to be finding a bench in the park in late October on a cold, drizzly evening to get his fix.

'Well, aye, there is, mate, there's behind the baths just down the road there, by the heaters like. But Christ, you're only a young lad, what you doing out here? Why aren't you in the homeless shelter?'

'You know how it is, mate.'

'Aye... Well, if you stay on the streets round here, you better have your wits about you! If you got anything to nick, they'll have it off you, the others. Take my advice and keep all your belongings, everything that's important to you like, hidden away, and if you can, whatever you do, don't go to sleep by them.'

'Thanks,' said Dave. 'But what do you do if you do need to sleep?'

'You don't. Not unless you get a bed in the shelter when it all gets too much, like.'

Don't go to sleep? Dave was shattered. The one thing that he needed to do was to go to sleep. He couldn't stay here, it was too cold. As the man continued to obtain his fix, Dave moved from the bench and began to walk down the road in the direction of the swimming baths.

Once he got there, he walked around the back of the building. There were a few people gathered around an old metal bin with a fire inside it. They eyed him suspiciously as he walked past. By now, Dave was so cold that he didn't care who saw him. At least this area felt warm, warmer than the rest of the town. Plus it had the advantage of being under cover. The prime positions close to the heat source had been taken - the regular occupants had staked their claims. The floor was covered in sleeping bags and other battered camping paraphernalia. What he would give for one of those sleeping bags! Dave sat on a concrete slab some way away from where the others were congregated. He didn't look at or speak to anyone.

Dave was alone. He hadn't been this cold at night since he was six years old, but at least back then, he'd had Ken and his nan. Bad thoughts began to whir in his head as he thought back. How he wished he was with them now. Tears began to roll down his cheeks. After a time, he felt his eyes begin to droop and he dared to lie down on the concrete floor. It was uncomfortable, but it was dry, and he was no longer saturated. He put his money in his plastic wallet with his other important things and hid it in his trouser leg where anyone trying to remove it would surely wake him first. Dave drifted in and out of consciousness for a short time. Then, despite fighting it, he drifted off to sleep. But he snapped awake when he felt something touching him. A man was trying to put his hand in Dave's pockets. He jumped up.

'You, do one and leave me alone, do I look like I've got anything to rob?'

'Alright, yeah, OK, sorry, mate, just, er, checking you were OK...'

'I said do one! Stay away from me, and I'll stay away from you!'

The man shrugged and slunk off to join those still congregated around the fire pit. Awakened by the commotion, they looked up to see what was happening. Dave couldn't stay here again; tomorrow, he needed to stay somewhere else. The streets were a dangerous place. If he stayed too long, he would undoubtedly get done over by someone, or become that desperate that he too would start taking something to forget, about everything, or even worse, just lose any hope that he ever had. He sat bolt upright, sure that he wouldn't dare to sleep again for the remainder of the night, eyeing the others with suspicion as they huddled around the fire. Soon, one by one, they drifted off to sleep. As the early hours of the morning drew in and once he was certain that the others were asleep, he could keep his eyes open no longer and he drifted off for an hour or so, waking back up again what seemed like five minutes later.

After being on the concrete all night, his bones ached and his back was stiff. He peeled himself off the floor, sparked up a cigarette and walked into town. It was a morose, chilly day, but at least the rain had stopped. Realising that he couldn't walk around much longer like this, unkempt, dressed in the same clothes, he bought himself some toothpaste, a brush and toiletries, together with a sandwich, water and snacks for his lunch. He went a cafe to get himself some breakfast. After he had eaten his fry up and drunk his coffee, he felt slightly more human.

'Can I have another coffee, please?' he asked the lady behind the counter.

Dave realised that he would need all the stimulation that he could get to make it through. He had a wash in the sink in the toilet and brushed his teeth.

Looking slightly more presentable, he made his way back to the building site. By ten o'clock, he was shattered. All he could do was push through and carry on. Realising that it was unfeasible to stay awake every night for much longer, he needed a plan. After what seemed like a lifetime, it was time to stop for lunch. Dave sat eating the sandwich that he had bought from the shop.

'Posh butties there, mate, you won the pools or somat!' asked one of the other lads.

'Na,' said Dave, 'just moved up here. I haven't got a kitchen at my place. In fact, don't suppose you know of any rooms to rent, do you? It's just, the place I'm in, it's dead cold and noisy like... I couldn't sleep all last night.'

'Yeah, there's always rooms up the road at the hotel outside the garage on the right. Bit shabby, but there's always rooms there. We got another twenty minutes on break yet, mate, why don't you go and ask now? You'll be there in two minutes.'

'Yeah? I'll go and have a look now, ta!'

The "hotel" was a once grand, turn-of-the-century building situated in a rather decrepit-looking street. If you didn't know that it was there, you wouldn't notice the hand-written sign outside advertising rooms to rent. Dave knocked on the heavy old door, the paintwork faded and flaking away. A skinny lady with short brown hair and a lined face, holding a cigarette, opened the door.

'Can I help you?'

'Yeah, I'm looking for a room to rent for a few nights. I don't suppose you've got anything, have you?'

She looked him up and down suspiciously. Seeing that he was dressed in work clothing, she beckoned for him to come in.

'Cheapest one I've got is five pound a night or twenty pound a week, money upfront, no visitors, front doors get locked at ten.'

'No problem.'

'I'll show you round.'

She led Dave through the old Victorian house. It was draughty and cold, but it was a house. A slight amount of heat was kicked out of the ancient cast iron radiators sparsely dotted around, making it less cold than outside. She led him up the once grand staircase, now missing spindles, to a poky single room at the top of the house.

'This is the cheapest one, twenty a week, you'll have to share the kitchen and the bathroom, or I've got one with a bathroom for thirty.'

The kitchen was more of a broom cupboard where there was a kettle, a toaster, cooker and a microwave. This would do. The bathroom looked as if it hadn't been altered since the beginning of the century.

'I'll take this one.'

She looked up at him.

'You sure? The other one's better…'

Dave wasn't looking for better. He was looking for somewhere that he could lie down at night, and hide away from the world when he finished work. And maybe he would only be here for a few nights until the police caught up with him. Then hopefully he would get sent to young offenders. Or maybe, just maybe, if he kept doing what he was doing, and got his head down, and kept himself to himself there was a faint chance that he could just carry on dodging them? Plus, what if he did manage to evade them and he was rained off all week at work? He needed the cheapest room possible. If he just went back and forth to work around the corner, there was a small chance that he would be able to get by under the radar without anybody noticing. He didn't quite have enough money left. He would need to collect his wages for the day before he could pay the whole amount.

'I'll take it for the week. I'll be getting paid later; any chance I can give you fifteen now and five later?'

She nodded reluctantly and handed him the key.

On his way back to the site, he passed a second hand shop. He didn't have long left on his break. Desperate for a change of clothes, Dave went in, picked up five random t-shirts in his size, a pair of jeans and a warm jumper to use for work.

The afternoon dragged. At times, Dave felt as if he would drop off to sleep while standing. His adrenaline soon kicked back in after he almost tipped over a wheelbarrow full of bricks, narrowly missing his feet. If he was to continue working here, in addition to sleep he would need to get himself some steel toe-capped boots.

That evening, he made his way back to the hotel. Using the last of his energy, he dragged himself into the shop on the way and bought some supplies to make sandwiches for the rest of the week. If he got laid off at any point, at least he could save his money from this week to pay his rent. Then he would have a bit of time to make another plan. He paid the landlady the outstanding money that he owed her and made his way up the stairs to his room.

Dave ate his tea. The shower in the bathroom didn't work so he filled the bath up. The water was lukewarm, but it didn't matter, he felt the cleanest that he had ever felt in his life. He scrubbed himself and washed his hair. The suds fell off him like the bad memories of the last few years. Afterwards, he realised that he didn't have a towel to dry himself. He brushed his teeth and let the water drip off him then crept out into the corridor, looking first to ensure that nobody was around. His room was cold and draughty, but Dave didn't care. The fact was that he had a room. He used one of the t-shirts that he had bought to dry himself off. He had a bed. He was clean, he had food, and clothes to wear. And most importantly, he was safe. Two days ago, he had had none of these things. In this shabby, draughty room in the middle of an unfamiliar town, he felt as if he was in heaven. How he hoped that the police would not choose tonight to come knocking on his door, then he could get a good sleep.

Early next morning, he sat bolt upright with a jump. Where was he? Was he still in the home? Was he behind the baths in town? Should he be sleeping? No! It was OK, it was all OK! He was here, nobody was chasing him, nobody was following him.

'Morning, Steve,' said the boss, when he arrived at the site. 'Blimey, you look better than you did yesterday. I thought we'd finished you off?'

Dave shook his head.

'Na,' he said. 'Got sorted in a new gaff; I wasn't getting any sleep in the other one.'

The foreman raised his eyebrows at him. Dave got onto the bricks and began carrying them up the ramp towards the buildings. Today, he felt invigorated. Work was nothing that he couldn't manage.

Two weeks later, Dave was sixteen. Still nobody had come looking for him. Now that he was safe and no longer preoccupied with getting from day to day, now he had his accommodation and basic needs sorted, he could stop worrying about being cold, or hungry, or soaking wet. With every day that passed, Dave looked over his shoulder a little less. But now he had time to think. Too much time. He hated this time of year, his birthday always reminded him of what had happened to his mum. Other kids looked forwards to their birthdays. No matter how special his nan or the people who were looking after him tried to make it, he just didn't like it. His birthday, this time of year reminded him of bad things; his nan, his mum, the homes, Ken, his dad, and he realised something else; he was alone. He was sixteen years old, sitting in a bedsit with nothing but a packet of cigarettes for company. He had nobody in the whole world to share anything with. Except Ken; he needed to go and see him, if just to see his face, to hug him, for Ken to tell him that everything would be OK, to validate him, Dave, as a person, to make him remember that he was someone, that he had come from somewhere, that he was once loved. Dave made his way across town to Ken's flat.

'Ken, it's me, Dave.'

The door opened. Ken put his arms around Dave and held him tightly.

'Dave!'

How right it felt to be in his brother's arms, to be with someone he belonged to, somebody who cared about him and loved him, and knew him. Dave felt his body relax, and butterflies began to pour out of his stomach.

'Ken, you can't tell anyone I've been here. I've run away. I've been living in town.'

'What?' said Ken. 'Why didn't you come here? Why didn't you tell me?'

'This is the first place that they're gonna look. Has anyone been round here? Asking about me? Or looking for me?'

Ken shook his head. 'No, mate.'

The flat was chaotic. But Dave didn't care. That afternoon, he sat in Ken's flat drinking beer and chatting to his brother, as if he had never been apart from him, as if everything was OK and normal. And that felt good, and nice, if only for a short time.

In reality, the fact was that everything was far from normal. Ken was chilled, too chilled, as if he didn't have a care in the world. Ken was happy, too happy. Ken was too positive, everything was 'cool' and 'groovy'. Then it became clear.

'Want some brown?'

'Eh?' asked Dave.

'Some smack? Go on, a birthday present, give it a try; it'll make you forget about everything.'

Heroin. Dave looked up at Ken, at his sallow skin and pin-prick pupils that prevented anyone being able to look into his soul, to see who he really was, what he was really thinking and feeling. His false sense of security, the flat, the chaos around him. Ken acted as if he had missed Dave. Dave was sure that he had. But in reality, Ken was entirely focussed the new love of his life: heroin. The truth was that his brother was on a downward trajectory which would undoubtedly, if left to continue, lead to a very bad outcome. Not in the least bit tempted and recalling the promise that he had made to his nan, Dave declined.

'No, mate, not for me, ta.'

'Go on, just try a hit…'

'No, mate, besides, I promised our nan I'd never do it.'

And just for that one moment, Ken looked ashamed, sad, as if there was a glimmer of insight into what he was doing, what he had become. But before long, Ken pulled a needle and syringe out of a drawer and began to heat a spoon over a candle. Unable to sit and watch him do it, realising that slowly but surely he was losing his brother, Dave decided that it was time to leave.

Over the next few weeks, Dave began to wonder if anybody was looking for him at all. He had passed a couple of policemen once or twice in the street; they hadn't looked twice at him. Weeks turned into months. Nobody came. Eventually, he stopped caring.

****

A few months later, the job on the building site came to an end. Dave applied for another job on another site. But this time it was for a big company, and he was on the payroll. He needed to have a bank account. He would need his national insurance number. Luckily he had his birth certificate. Dave realised that if he had a bank account, and gave an address, he could be traceable; this would surely flag him up on the systems of an authority together with his last known address. But if he was to continue to live a normal life, he couldn't live under the radar forever. Now, he even went by his real name. Still - nobody came looking for him.

At last, he felt safe walking around town which he frequently did. He often went out with Ken, and on nights out with some of the lads from the site and to some of the football matches in town. He and Ken had even ventured on the train to Manchester to watch Man City playing. Then, eighteen months after he had run away, walking through town, he heard a familiar voice.

'Dave! How are you?'

Dave spun round. It was Penny, his old social worker! His first instinct was to run.

'Where have you been? I've been worried sick about you!'

For some reason, Dave's heart stopped beating as fast. There was something about her demeanour, something innocent and naïve. It was as if she was genuinely pleased to see him - almost relieved, non-confrontational. He'd expected her to be shocked when she saw him, at least frightened of him after what he had done to Blackwell and Evans... maybe she was going to try and persuade him to hand himself in?

'I'm... I'm OK, ta.'

Dave stood, awkwardly waiting for her to advise him to do the right thing and hand himself in to the police. Or that they wanted to see him in the home. Or something...

'I phoned up to speak to you, and they told me that you'd run away! I've been worried sick about you! I looked everywhere; they told me that even your brother hadn't seen you!'

'I, er, I just left. I didn't like it there.'

'But why, Dave?'

She asked without blinking, or looking shifty, or turning away. Clearly she had no idea why Dave had hated it that much that he had bolted at the first opportunity. She didn't know what had happened in the wood shed. Nobody had told her. And nobody had come looking for him at Ken's flat!

'Even the police didn't know you were missing when I phoned them…'

There was only one explanation - they didn't want the police there, asking questions, investigating anything. They hadn't reported the incident to the police or any other authorities - they had covered the whole thing up! He had spent the last year and a half worrying that he was being pursued, hunted, traced. Already lost in the care system, Dave wasn't missed by anyone. Besides, apart from Ken, who didn't even know what day it was, who else would care where he had gone? Who would come looking for him?

'Where did you go?'

'Just to town. There was no way I was staying there...'

'But why did you run away?'

Dave didn't reply. He just put his head down.

'Dave?'

'Just do me one favour?'

'Yes, of course I will, if I can.'

'Next time you need to put a kid in a care home, make sure that it's never in one run by Reginald Evans or where Leslie Blackwell is working.'

She looked up at him with a knowing look in her eyes.

'Look,' she said changing her tone and shifting around uncomfortably, 'I've heard that there's been a few things happening up there, Dave, things that people aren't happy about. Did something happen to you?'

Dave wanted to tell her, but he didn't want to talk about it, it made him have to remember. And what if they were still after him? Dave put his head down again and didn't reply.

'Dave? If it did, would you be prepared to speak to the police about it?'

No, not the police! As long as he didn't bump into Blackwell or Evans or ever have to see them again, or have to talk about them, Dave felt safe. Much as he wanted to trust her, he just couldn't believe that Blackwell and Evans were operating alone. Surely kids had complained about them before? Kids that he knew that were also in care had been telling him about things that happened in care homes for years and it was still going on now. How could the police not know? How could she have never known? What if she was in on it all?

'No, I don't want to. I just want them all to leave me alone, and I'll be fine.'

Penny pursed her lips. 'OK, Dave. I understand. Well, if you need me again, for anything, you know where to find me, don't you?'

Instantly a weight was lifted off Dave's shoulders as he realised something. He was safe to carry on living his life, free. He no longer had to worry about being found, because nobody was looking for him. He no longer had to worry about being chased, because nobody was hunting for him. If they knew that he had said something, maybe they'd find out where he lived? And come looking for him? No, if he stayed away from them and left them alone, maybe they'd leave him alone. That was the best that he could hope for.

'Yeah, thanks anyway, see you around.'

'Goodbye, Dave. But remember, I'm still your social worker. Until you're eighteen. So you may well be hearing from me again.'

'Look, I'm, I'm OK. I'm fine, I don't need any help now, thanks anyway.'

'Well, are you going to at least tell me where you live?'

Dave shook his head. 'No, sorry,' he said as he walked away. She stood and watched him go.

****

A few weeks later, just after he had arrived home from work, there was a knock at his door.

'Dave Williams? It's the police. Can we come in and ask you a few questions?'

Dave froze. Had they finally caught up with him? Had Blackwell and Evans reported him for assaulting them with an axe? Were they going to arrest him? Would he have to see them? Were they real policemen? What if they were just two of their accomplices dressed up as policemen? Sent by Blackwell, Evans and whoever else was in their gang? What if it was Blackwell and Evans? He didn't answer.

'Look, mate, we know you're in there, the landlady's just told us she's seen you come in.'

Blasted Miss Crapper! It was no good, he couldn't ignore them, hoping they would just go away.

'You got any ID?' Dave heard a walkie talkie go off and a call come in – it was definitely the police.

'Yes, mate, but I suppose you'll have to open the door for us to show you really.'

Reluctantly, Dave opened the door. Two policemen stood there.

'Er, what's it all about?'

'Well, it's a bit sensitive really. It's about the time that you spent in care, more specifically about some people that may have looked after you. Can we come in?'

Dave nodded reluctantly and opened the door wider. His hand shook as he slammed it shut. He had been dreading this moment for nearly two years.

'It's about the time that you spent in the home up the road, about the time you spent there in care. Basically, we're investigating claims that some of the staff may have been, well, not very nice to some of the children who lived there.'

Dave's heart sank. He looked down, attempting to avert the gaze of the police officer. His heart began to pound in his chest as the memories that he had tried so hard to forget came flooding back into his head, like a dam that had burst. As he looked up at the police, Blackwell and Evans' faces became superimposed on theirs. Dave looked away. He sat down on his bed and looked at the floor instead. Paranoia began to set in; what if these rozzers were in on it all? Friends of Blackwell and Evans? They took him through the usual police spiel of what would happen to any evidence that he gave and so on.

'So I need to ask you, at any time, during the time that you lived in the noted children's home, did you feel threatened or were you harmed by any of the staff that worked there?' asked one of the police officers as the other one scribbled in a notebook.

Unable to meet the gaze of the police officers, Dave shook his head. 'No.'

'At any time during the time that you lived there were you threatened or harmed by anyone outside the home?'

Why on earth were they asking him that? To be fair, Dave hadn't been threatened or harmed by anyone outside of the home. What did they mean? What else was going on there?

'No.'

The policemen looked at Dave and looked at each other. Dave could tell they weren't convinced he was telling the truth.

'At any time during the time that you lived there were you assaulted in a physical manner?'

Dave paused then shook his head and lowered his gaze again. He wasn't quite sure why, but tears began to spill out of his eyes. He had tried so hard to forget this, to put it behind him, to move on with his life. He shook his head.

The policeman paused.

'What about in a sexual manner?'

Dave shook his head again. This confirmed his worst fears - that must have been what was happening to the other lads there. What about Ken? He put his head in his hands.

'So, David, what you're telling me is that you never had any of the members of staff causing you any physical or sexual harm? It's OK, take your time…'

Yeah, they knew that he was lying. But if he refused to say anything, surely they couldn't do anything about it? Dave looked back up and shook his head slowly. 'No.'

'Did you ever see anyone in the home abusing any of the other children in a physical, emotional or sexual manner?'

Dave paused as he thought back to the other boys, Dennis, Matthew and Marlon. He shook his head.

'No.'

Silent tears dripped down his face. Dave wasn't sure why. He felt out of control, and under pressure. These questions about the home, they were all way out of his comfort zone. The policemen looked at each other again. It was clear that Dave was lying. One of them handed him a tissue.

'David, is there anything else that you want to tell us? That you think that we ought to know?'

Wiping the tears away, Dave shook his head again. Could he trust these policemen? A wave of vengeance came over him and Dave desperately wanted to tell them things, about what had happened, not even to him, but to the other lads. But he just couldn't bring himself to do it. He just wanted them to leave, to leave him alone. How had they known where to find him?

'No. But how did you know where I lived?'

'Well, your social worker, Penny Watts, felt that we should speak to you. She said that she had always been led to believe that you had just "disappeared" while living at the home but she was shocked to find you in the middle of town the other week.'

His social worker! Had she sent them round out of concern? Or to weigh him up? To see if he would talk or not?

'We traced you through the council tax; you're registered as living here.'

'Do they know where I live?'

The two policemen looked at each other. 'Who, David?' Dave looked up.

'Blackwell and Evans, from the home.'

They looked at each other again knowingly. 'No, Dave, this is confidential. Look, are you sure you don't want to tell us anything? If there is anything that you want to tell us, you need to tell us now.'

By now he had stopped crying. Eventually he shook his head.

The policemen looked at each other. One pulled out a piece of paper and scribbled on it. 'If you do remember anything that you want to tell us, give me a ring.' He handed the piece of paper to Dave.

'Yeah, thanks,' said Dave as he saw them out. As soon as he had shut the door, Dave screwed the piece of paper into a ball and threw it aside. He sank to the floor in shock: people knew where he lived - he had to get out of there!

Shortly after they had left, Miss Crapper came knocking at the door.

'Steve? Or is it Dave? I've just had two policemen here looking for you, saying that your name is Dave! You'd better not be bringing any trouble to my establishment.' Dave composed himself and stood up to open the door.

'It's nothing to do with me, it's to do with someone I know, alright?'

'Well, you better not be doing anythin' dodgy, not from here.'

Dave began to laugh.

'Do I look like I'm doing anything dodgy? Have I ever brought people round here? Or do you need to come knocking at my door every five minutes to warn me about breaking rules?'

'Well no, but after you've lived here for over a year, I still don't know anything about you. So if you've got the police knocking…'

'Why should you know anything about me? You're my landlady, not my mother.'

'No, but you hide away in here, you haven't even got a girlfriend, how do I know…'

'What are you trying to say, Miss Crapper?'

'Well, it's just not normal is...'

'How the hell do you know? You don't know anything about me.'

Miss Crapper! She was just like the rest of them. Suspicious, judging him, having him down for being nothing but a criminal. A good for nothing – weird and odd with criminal tendencies! Well, he'd tell her!

'Yeah? Well, you can shove your room! I ain't staying here to be spoken to like that by you. Who do you think you are?'

'Well, there's no need...'

'No, you can sod off, judging me like that! My life's been hard enough as it is without you poking your nose into it. For your information, they were asking me about what the staff were like when I was in care.'

Mrs Crapper's face dropped.

'Why do you think I rocked up here? At fifteen years old? Renting one of your draughty, crappy rooms? Because it was that bad I could stand living there. To be honest, I only stayed here because you didn't ask where I'd come from.'

'Look, Steve... I mean Dave, I...'

'You're just like the rest of them. So don't you worry, Miss Crapper, I'll be out of your room tomorrow. And for your information, my name's not even Steve, it's Dave.'

'Well look, you don't have to go... I'm just saying that...'

'Shove your room! Tomorrow, I'm out of here.'

April 1989

The next day, Dave packed his stuff and moved in with Ken for a few days until he could sort out somewhere else to live. By now, Ken had been evicted from his flat and was living in a squat in town. Living with Ken in a squat was the last thing that Dave wanted to do. He had saved up a bit of money and planned to move at some point, but not yet. He really wished he hadn't had his outburst at Miss Crapper, but Dave wasn't very good at swallowing his pride. It came from a life in care; once the little trust and faith he had in anything had gone there was no possibility of restoration. He took a deep breath as he carted his luggage through the streets, fully suspecting that he was jumping out of the frying pain into the fire.

Being an outsider from Manchester with no family connections except for Ken, Dave had initially found it hard to fit in in the new town in North Wales. But over the last year or so, he had got used to the place. It was smaller than Manchester. Nobody knew him, or knew anything about his past. He felt safe and relaxed. He had enquired about a couple of bedsits and was hopefully moving into one in the next couple of weeks. In the meantime, he had nowhere else to go.

Every time he visited, Ken's chaotic surroundings were becoming increasingly geared around his habit. He made no secret of the needles left lying around, with dirty spoons, foil, and other paraphernalia. They were becoming as commonplace as the everyday household items that Dave used such as his kettle, plates and ashtrays. As Ken became more dependent, he became more open, as if daily use was normal. People came and went. Dave never got to know most of them by name. Some of them were other lads that he recognised from the care system. For the most part, he and Ken never discussed what had happened. It was too painful to talk about. Besides, when he was taking heroin, despite being off his face, Ken was happy.

Living in a squat wasn't easy. It only took Dave a few hours to reach the point where he wished that he hadn't fallen out with Miss Crapper. For a working person not reliant on drugs, living with people on heroin was not compatible with a normal lifestyle. When he came home from work, Dave wanted sanctuary and solitude. He couldn't cope with the chaotic scenes that greeted him, the fights, the arguments, the door being barged down by the police. Giving the people that came demanding money they were owed by Ken meant that he had little money left for himself. There were people coming and going all through the night, and weekends, especially, were noisy. Some of his clothes and stuff had gone missing, he had nowhere to put anything: he just wanted to be on his own.

It had all come to head one evening when his new jacket had gone missing. It was the one in which he kept his important stuff in the plastic wallet. He usually slept in it and took it to work so that he could keep an eye on it, but when he had gone downstairs to make a cup of tea, it had gone. There was only him, Ken and another guy called Russ there. He had let things that had happened in the squat go in the past, but not this time.

'Russ, give me frigging coat back; it's got pictures of my nan and our mum in there.'

'Er, uh, I dunno what you're talking about mate, sorry…'

'Now, Russ, I'm not joking. I'd do time in prison for that coat.'

'Sorry, Dave, I dunno what…'

Dave grabbed Russ by his collar and shoved him onto the floor.

'Now! The coat, Russ! Give it back to me before I knock your block off!'

'Mate, I honestly dunno what…'

'Alright, alright,' said Ken. 'Leave it, Dave, let him go!'

'Are you joking? He's robbed me coat!'

'Mate… he hasn't.'

'No, he has, well, who else could it have…' Something was beginning to dawn on Dave. 'You?'

Dave pulled Russ up off the floor.

'Russ, I'm sorry, mate, I'm really sorry. You?' He turned to Ken. Ken put his head down.

'Ken, are you really that far gone, you'd rob off your own brother? I've been bailing you out for months! Paying your debts! Making sure you eat, and this is how you repay me?'

'Sorry, mate… I just...'

Dave grabbed Ken's shoulders and pulled him roughly towards him.

'How could you? It shouldn't be like this! It should be you looking after me, you should have looked after me, got me out of that home! You chose this over me! This crap! Living like this…'

'I… I… I'm sorry, Dave…'

'Yeah, coz that's all you give a crap about, innit? Another hit, Ken? What about me? What about me? And our nan? There's pictures of her in there, it's all I've got left!'

'I'm, I'm sorry, Dave…'

'You should be, you're not my brother! The only person you give a toss about, is yourself! You ain't no brother to me! Now, give me my coat, now!'

Ken pulled up one of the rancid cushions on the sofa and pulled Dave's jacket out from underneath. Dave angrily grabbed it off him and checked the pockets. He had had a five-pound note in the pocket, it had gone. That didn't bother him. The plastic wallet with all his things in was still in the large pocket at the back.

That evening Dave packed his things and went to stay in a hotel up the road for a few days until his bedsit was ready. He realised that he was fighting a losing battle trying to help Ken and that heroin was prioritised even over him. Much as he hated to admit it, Dave realised that Ken was beyond any help. While he still supported him, Dave knew that he had to get away from his brother before he was dragged down into the mire.

February 1990

Dave had been allocated a council flat on the estate on the outskirts of town. Everyone in town thought that area was rough, but it was nothing compared to the estate where Dave and Ken used to live: it didn't even have any high rises above three storeys! And if you sat on the hill opposite, you could see to the other end of it. If you looked out of the top of the highest high rise on Dave's old estate you could never see where the estate began and ended for the sea of council houses and flats that stretched for miles around. In this place, the people were OK, they were friendly once you got to know them and they knew that you were OK. It had its problems like anywhere else. Where he came from, if you owed someone money or annoyed them you'd get shot or stabbed. Here, you'd get a smack in the face, possibly a chipped tooth or a broken rib at worst.

One Saturday morning, Dave went to see Ken in the squat. He opened the door and walked into a haze of smoke. It was the usual post-Friday night scenario. Bodies lay on the floor, some passed out, some in a daze. Dave found Ken lying amongst them on the filthy tattered couch in the corner.

'Ken, it's me, Dave, come on, I'll get you a fry up'.

'Eh? OK.'

'When did you last eat?'

'Aw, I, er dunno.'

There was not an ounce of fat left on Ken. If he had money, his priority would be to buy himself drugs over anything else. There was no point in buying him food as he would just sell it or forget to eat it. So every few days, to prevent him becoming dehydrated or starving, Dave would take him out to buy him something to eat. Then they would go to the cinema, or the pub, and chat about their nan and the old days, just for a few hours, so that they could both feel normal again.

At the café, Dave went to the counter to order them both a large full English breakfast and a cup of tea.

And there she was, behind the counter, with the largest, brightest, shiniest eyes that he had ever seen, with the longest eyelashes and dark, silky smooth hair tied up in a bobble on the top of her head – Audrey Hawkins. Her eyes met his; it was love at first sight.

'Two full English's, and your phone number please.' Dave ran his hand through his hair. 'And if you don't give it to me,' he added, leaning on the counter, 'I'm just gonna come back here every week until you change your mind!'

March 1990

The next Saturday, Dave had arranged to meet Audrey at a pub in town. It was a beautiful March evening, the kind of evening where for the first time after the long winter, summer could be felt trying its best to signal to the earth from the sky up above. Feeling apprehensive, Dave fully expected her not to turn up. The pub was loud, and noisy. He gasped as she walked in, her shiny long brown hair draped around her shoulders, and her big doe eyes peeping from underneath her lashes. She wore leggings and flat, green, thigh-length boots. How glad Dave was - she was nearly as tall as him.

'Audrey,' said Dave, standing up to go and meet her. 'You came then?'

Audrey nodded. 'I told you I would.'

'Can I get you a drink?' asked Dave, realising that he had been staring at her for far too long.

Dave bought her a glass of wine. He felt as if he was walking on air; she had come, she had actually come! They sat down, and Dave couldn't think of a thing to say. Not because he didn't want to talk to her, but because he was so in awe of her that he couldn't stop staring at her.

'So, er, how was your day?'

'Fine,' she replied, shyly.

And they sat there for a while, in uncomfortable silence. Eventually, Dave spoke.

'Sorry, Audrey, I can't stop staring at you,' he said, feeling that he had to be honest. If he didn't tell her the truth, he feared she would think he was some kind of weirdo. She began to giggle.

'No, honest, Audrey, I can't... I really can't!'

'I like your voice... where are you from?'

'Manchester.'

At first, every time he talked, she kept looking up at him and giggling. He grinned at her. The pub was noisy. Dave wished that he could hear her better, but then felt glad that he couldn't because it meant that he had to sit closer to her. He liked her, very much.

'So what was it like there? Did you like it?'

'No, not really.'

'Why?'

'It was too big, and I don't know anyone there anymore.'

'I don't like big places, or busy ones.'

'What, like pubs?'

'Er… well, they're OK.'

They finished their drinks. So Audrey didn't like busy places, or seem to like pubs. Neither did Dave. He racked his brains to think of somewhere else that he could take her. *Where would she like to go?* He was just about to ask her if she wanted another one, and glanced up at the bar to ensure that it was not too busy, when he saw something that made his stomach turn and his skin crawl.

Leslie Blackwell! Standing at the bar, drinking, a stick by his side. Alone. Dave began to feel palpitations rising in his chest. Beads of cold sweat formed on his forehead and dripped down his face. Vivid flashbacks intruded into his mind. Audrey was chatting away to him about something and didn't appear to notice that he was preoccupied. He felt his heart race faster; *he had to get out of here, he had to get out, he had to go, now! But wait! He was with Audrey! If he just left, she would think that he was strange.*

Eventually realising that something was wrong, she stopped talking and looked around the pub.

'Dave, are you OK?'

'Er, Audrey, do you mind if we go somewhere else?'

'Well, no,' she replied. 'Where are you thinking?'

'Come out with me, and I'll tell you.'

He led her outside, relief sweeping through his body.

As he stepped into the fresh air, his heart stopped racing, the flashbacks ceased and his breathing rate slowed down. Questions ran through his head. Why had he just left? Blackwell was standing at the bar, with a stick! What was he going to do? What was he going to say? Plus, Blackwell was alone! He couldn't do anything! Surely he would have been more scared of Dave than Dave was of him. Damn, why had he walked out of there? Why hadn't he stayed? He was sick of running and hiding, from nothing! It wasn't even him that should be running! Now what?

'Well, where did you want to go?' asked Audrey.

Dave had no idea. He didn't frequent the pubs in town that often, he didn't know what any of them were called. Most of the ones that he went to with his workmates weren't places that he would take someone like Audrey. Should they walk into town? No! That was a bad idea; what if he saw Blackwell in another pub and got freaked out? He couldn't just keep leaving. Dave looked around in desperation. Then he looked up and saw somewhere that he really wanted to go with Audrey.

'Well,' said Dave, 'er, Audrey, this might sound weird, but I've always wanted to go up that hill there, you know, to the top? The one at the bottom of that mountain? I reckon we might have time to climb it before it gets dark. Then I can take you for something to eat, if you'd like? I mean, you don't have to, only if you'd like to.'

Audrey looked up at him and her mouth dropped open. 'What? You want to walk up there?'

'Well, er… yeah.'

Audrey stood and started at him for a while. 'You don't… you're not going to try anything on are you, up there?'

Dave laughed, then his expression changed to one of seriousness. 'No, what do you think I am? I mean… of course not, I just, er… can't hear you very well in the pub. That's all. I want to talk to you. Properly. And I noticed you've got flat shoes on.'

Dave's body flooded with relief as Audrey smiled at him.

'OK, do you know the way?'

'Er, no, will you show me?'

She led him towards the path to the hills.

'Do you like walking, Dave?'

'Yes.'

It was true, he did like walking. He enjoyed going for long rambling walks where he could forget everything and explore, and look at the grass and the trees and the hills. Where he was unlikely to bump into anyone that he knew from the past. Walking made him forget things.

'Me too.'

After a climb, they sat at the top of the hill. The view was astounding. In front of them, Dave could see right over town, to the beginning of the estate and the end, the hospital, the houses, the landmarks in the centre of town, over to the beginning of the dual carriageway leading out of town and the industrial estates beyond. From up here, the world was smaller. Manageable somehow. Then behind them, there was nothing, just fields, leading to the mountains, paradise stretching out for miles and miles around.

'So, Dave, how did you end up living here?'

Dave put his head down. What should he say? Not expecting her to turn up, he had not mentally prepared himself for what would happen if she did, for what he should and should not tell her. But what if she wanted to see him again? How could he lie? Dave took a deep breath.

'Well… me and my brother Ken, we used to live in Manchester with our nan after our mum died. Then Nan died. So we ended up in a care home around here, then I just kind of stayed.'

Trying to downplay his life in care as much as he could and just stick to the facts, Dave only revealed the tip of the very deep iceberg that was the care system and the experience that he had had of it. He hadn't talked about it all to anyone for years. He shuddered as he thought about it, using every force in his body to suppress the jitters that went through him at the mere mention of it.

'That must have been really hard. I'm sorry to hear that.'

'I've left now,' he said with a shrug, all the time wracking his brains to try and think of the best way to change the subject. 'Anyway, what about you, Audrey? Are you from here, originally?'

'I've lived here all my life.'

'I've never been to this part of the hills before. I like it.'

'Nice, isn't it? The view from up the mountain behind is even better; I would show you it, but it would be dark by the time we got up to the top.'

'Will you take me there one day?'

Audrey nodded. Dave wondered if maybe she was just being polite.

'Anyway, hadn't we better go back down? Before it gets dark and all that? Before I turn into a vampire and try to drink your blood or something?

Audrey grinned at him as she got up. They began to walk back down. Dave wanted to grab her hand, but he didn't dare.

'Do you think you'll stay here, Dave? I bet you find it a bit boring compared to Manchester.'

Oh, not again. *Just be honest Dave, you've got to trust someone*.

'Well, I, er, I, na, not really. It's too big there for me. Plus, my brother stayed round here after he left care too, and I have to, well, look after him.'

'Why? What's wrong with him?'

'He's only a year and a bit older than me, he lives in a squat in town, he… he takes drugs. So I try to look out for him. That's why I've ended up staying round here really. I take him to the café sometimes.'

'Really? The boy you come to the café with? That's your brother?' Audrey asked in disbelief. Dave nodded.

'Yeah, anyway, I've got no other close family, no other reason to go back really.'

There, he had said it. Now he waited. Waited for her to judge him like other people did. He was just a kid, with no one except a brother who was addicted to heroin. A kid with no qualifications, who had just left care and lived in a flat in a rough area of town. Who had a brother who lived in a squat. Undoubtedly from a bad background.

'Gosh! How old were you when you went into care?'

This was strange. Much as he hated talking about the past, Dave didn't mind talking to Audrey about it. He took a deep breath, not as deep as usual because she was easy to talk to; it felt, natural somehow, almost as if he was OK with it.

'Well, my mum died when I was six, then me and my brother lived with our nan until she died when I was fourteen. My nan was my mum as far as I was concerned. We don't see our dad. So we went to live in care. I hated the home, I lasted less than a week there.'

'That's really sad.'

Dave's heart sank. He didn't want her to feel pity for him. He just wanted her to like him.

'Yeah, I suppose it is. But it's a time of my life I've left behind. It's a time I'd rather try and forget, to be honest. I find it really hard to talk about it all usually.'

'Sorry, I didn't mean to…'

'No… no… I don't mind talking about it… to you.'

Dave wasn't finding it hard to talk to Audrey. He found himself wanting to tell her more. She was the kind of person who he would have loved to have been able to tell exactly why he had just left the pub, but he just could not bring himself to do so, not yet.

'All I've got is my brother; I suppose I've never thought of moving anywhere else because he's only nineteen and he's in a mess. I have to take him out and get him something to eat every now and again, otherwise he'd just never eat.'

Suddenly, Dave felt something, something warm in his hand. It was Audrey's hand as she grabbed his. His heart began to glow, and he felt all warm inside, just like he used to feel when his nan cuddled him. How he wanted to hold Audrey.

Dave stopped half way down the hill as they walked and stared at her. He cupped her face in his hands and pulled her in to him. She didn't push him away. He had made a promise to her, he just wanted to touch her. He stroked her hair, it was silky; her bright shiny eyes shone in the fading light.

'Told you I wouldn't try anything on up there, didn't I?' Dave said, smiling at her. 'Come on, I'd better get you somethin' to eat before you eat me.'

Dave took her to McDonald's. They talked, and talked, until eventually it was time to go home.

'So, can I see you again, Audrey?'

'Yes,' she said. 'Maybe next week, early one evening, I can show you the other mountain? One night after work? Or next weekend?'

She had said yes. That meant that she must like him! He had been only half-joking, he had never expected to see her again… not after he had told her about his background and his brother. And after he'd taken her out of the pub for a walk up the mountain!

'Yes, one night after work, I'm free any night. But why do you want to see me again?'

Oops, he hadn't meant to speak his thoughts aloud.

'Well, because I like you.'

'Do you?'

'Yes, I do. I liked just going for a walk, I don't really like going to crowded pubs and getting drunk… I just like doing normal things.'

A large grin spread across Dave's face. Leslie Blackwell had done him a favour. When and how had that ever happened? Now Audrey thought that he, Dave, was marvellous because he had taken her for a walk, which had been the most enjoyable walk that he had ever been on. And she wanted to see him again!

‘Or you could show me tomorrow?’ said Dave.

August 1990

At first, her family disapproved. Dave accepted it. At the end of the day, he had just turned up in town fresh from the care system with a dodgy family background and a brother in tow, who was a junkie living rough in a squat. Dave respected the fact that her family didn't approve – it meant that they cared about her. Audrey, on the other hand, never judged him for his past; she told him that it was only how he treated her that she cared about.

One day there was a knock at the door of his flat. Audrey's Dad.

'Mr. Hawkins.'

'There's £200 there!' he said as he handed Dave an envelope. 'Open it! Think of all the stuff that you can get with that! £200 to stay away from my daughter!'

Audrey's dad was not a rich man. The £200 was probably his life's savings. Dave looked him in the eye. He was perfectly serious and genuine. Dave folded his arms.

'Na, thanks.' Presuming that their business was done, he went to shut the door. Audrey's dad put his foot in it to stop him.

'OK, you want more? Final offer, £500? I'll get you the cash by next week! But that's all I can stretch to, if it's money you're after, I...'

Dave laughed. 'You don't get it do you, Mr. Hawkins?'

'Get what?'

'If you gave me two million pounds, I wouldn't keep away from her, not for any amount of money; she's priceless to me.'

Audrey's dad's face dropped. It was clear that this had not occurred to him.

'You're perfectly serious, aren't you?'

Dave laughed. He hadn't meant to laugh, and he certainly hadn't meant to disrespect Audrey's dad. The laugh had just escaped. Oh well, it was clear that Mr. Hawkins didn't like him anyway. What did he have him down for, offering him money to stay away from Audrey?

'Sorry, but you're gonna have to kill me to keep me away from her!'

Audrey's dad's eyes narrowed. He stared up at Dave, again for a prolonged amount of time and then he pointed his finger at him.

'If you ever mistreat my daughter, I will kill you.'

Dave smiled and shook his head, all the time staring straight into Mr. Hawkins' eyes.

'Mr. Hawkins, if I ever mistreat your daughter, I fully expect nothin' less!'

Mr. Hawkins nodded at him. 'Good, then we both understand each other, don't we?'

'We certainly do, or at least I hope that we do, so now you can keep your money where it belongs, in the bank.'

Eventually Mr. Hawkins' face creased into an odd and strange smile. He turned and walked away.

They got on after that. Dave and Audrey got married and moved into a council house on the estate. They had two beautiful girls. Everyone said that they needed to keep trying until they had a boy, but Dave was glad. He found men difficult to trust and hard to be around. They had let him down in the past, and it took him a long time to get to know them, to get used to them. He much preferred the company of women. In his house, with his girls, Dave felt safe and content. And on the rare occasion that anybody ever upset one of them, his wrath emerged.

True to his word he never once let Audrey down. Even now, nearly thirty years later, he looked at her, still wondering why it was that she was with him. Often he thought that he was in a dream and one day he was going to wake up. He may not have had the best start in life, but Dave Williams felt as if he had won the pools every time he looked at his family.

Friday December 20th 2019

'Evening, love,' said Audrey in a croaky voice as she burst in through the front door, panting. It was Friday, the end of her week-long cleaning stint in the factory. She didn't look well.

'Hiya, darlin'. How you feeling?'

This winter, Audrey had had the mother of all colds. No one could understand where it had come from. She was usually fit and well. Yet she had spent most of the month leading up to Christmas with a hacking cough, and feeling short of breath. She couldn't walk far and seemed to be getting worse, not better. Dave hated seeing her like this.

'You any better?'

She shook her head.

'Not really.'

'Well, you'll have to be better soon love, you can't be ill for much longer, can you? I can't have anything happening to you, what would I do without you?' He kissed her on the cheek. 'Look, why don't you just go on the sick?'

Audrey took in a deep breath.

'I should, love, but I dunno… what with you being rained off on the site this week, I just don't think I should. If I'm not better soon, I promise I'll go back to the doc's.'

'Well, it's nearly Christmas, you've worked hard all year. Have some time off, we'll manage! I've got savings, that's what I stash them for!'

'No, Dave, I'll be OK.'

'Seriously! Take some time off, love. You can't go to work like that, don't worry about us. We've got the house nearly paid off, most of the Christmas stuff, we'll manage!'

'I…I just feel weird! It's not like a normal cold. I can't breathe properly, and I couldn't even smell the bleach in work today, or taste my dinner!'

Anxiety began to build up in Dave, those same old feelings and thought processes that surfaced during the worst times of his childhood. The adverse experiences that he had encountered usually made him worry about loss and being out of control. This meant that he found uncertainty and worry difficult to deal with, especially when it came to his family. He associated illness with loss, and he couldn't cope with the prospect of anything terrible happening to Audrey. Over the years, he had learned that when illness or uncertain things happened, bad things usually followed. He craved certainty, and familiarity, and stability. For years he had had that. The rational part of him realised that she probably just had a cold and that she would be fine. But as much as he tried to stop feeling anxious, he couldn't.

'I'll book a taxi and we can go to A&E now?'

Audrey shook her head.

'No, I'm not that bad... loads of people are much worse off than me, Dave.'

'Well, book in with the docs, tomorrow.'

Over the years, Dave had learned to listen to his gut instinct. But when he got anxious, everything and everyone new became a threat with which he could not cope. And despite trying to rationalise it all, he had a weird feeling in the pit of his stomach that Audrey really wasn't well. He had been ruminating over it night and day and it was beginning to freak him out. He reached for his tobacco and roll up papers, just like he always did when he got stressed. Before he knew it, he had gone through half the pack.

A few years ago, he had read in the local paper that the police had successfully prosecuted members of a large paedophile ring working in local care homes. Blackwell and Evans' names were mentioned. He had breathed a sigh of relief knowing that they had gone to jail; Blackwell for ten years, Evans for twelve. As soon as he started reading some of the stories that the kids told, he had to stop reading - it was just too painful. He had seen some of them round town like Ken, on the downward trajectory into the mire. How else could they cope with life? They had seen and experienced too much; they would never be normal again. Sometimes Dave found it a struggle, and his life had been heaven compared to theirs.

After he had had the misfortune of reading about it in the paper, he had felt unwell for some weeks. It had manifested in him going off work sick and visiting the GP several times with chest pain, diarrhoea, weight loss and insomnia. Blood tests and a trace of his heart had found nothing of note. When he had got his head around it and started to make sense of it, he realised that he had been left with guilt. Guilt about not giving information to the police when they had asked him to do so, guilt about trying to forget about it all, but above all, guilt about the fact that the adverse experiences of his childhood had ruined his brother's life and not his. That just didn't seem fair.

Ken led a chaotic lifestyle where he had tried and failed several times to stop taking drugs. He took methadone, a heroin substitute which he had tried to reduce. For some periods of time, he would be OK. But it was as if the more normal and less addicted he became, the less he could handle the reality of life. The less under the influence of drugs he was, the more he remembered and dwelled on the past as it began to eat him away. Then he would relapse and start taking heroin again, stop paying his bills and get thrown out of wherever it was that he was living and he would be back to square one. At one time, Ken had even had a long-term girlfriend and they'd had a daughter. But it was as if he couldn't handle it, the pressure, the responsibility, the normality. While Dave revelled in it, it was as if it all felt too alien to Ken; he was always after that one more hit to try and forget. Dave tried his best to help him where he could, but much as he hated to admit it, he found being around his brother for any length of time difficult.

Dave had stayed where it was safe with his girls. Occasionally he would meet his mates in the pub to watch Man City playing or take Audrey to the social club on the estate. But he didn't go out much unless he went to work or out walking with Audrey. He enjoyed his work as a builder and he enjoyed having a laugh with the other lads, most of whom he had worked with for years. That was all Dave wanted from life; he was happy with his lot.

Then, last year, his back had started to ache every time he undertook any form of strenuous lifting and bending. When he was doing light duties, it wasn't too bad. But there weren't many jobs in building that were light duties. A few months ago, he had been carrying some bricks in a wheelbarrow up a ramp and his back had gone into an excruciatingly painful spasm. The first few times that it had happened, he had borrowed some of Audrey's dad's strong painkillers and just carried on through, but it was hard. He had gone back and it had happened again. Every time it happened, it was getting worse and worse. Dave didn't get paid if he didn't work. This time he had decided that enough was enough.

He wanted a job where he could keep mobile; he knew that he wouldn't like sitting still or standing in the same place all day. And he was sick of working outside. Eventually, he saw an advert for a job agency recruiting for the local hospital.

Monday December 23rd 2019

Audrey had been off work for two days. Her chest was tight. She was coughing and now she couldn't breathe properly. She had been to the doctors and they had said that they couldn't find anything wrong with her. But because she had a temperature of 39 degrees, they'd given her some antibiotics. Dave had suggested to her that she should go in to A&E, but she had refused.

As well as still trying to work, Dave had done everything else; food shopping – which had sent the palpitations in his chest into overdrive in the busy supermarket - written cards, sorted presents and put the decorations up. With Audrey being unwell, not being able to work and the pressure of Christmas, Dave was finding it hard.

'I'm only on the agency, so if I don't work, I don't get paid. I can't be ill for long, and you've got no work, then there's your back...'

'Don't worry, love, I've got it sorted.'

'How?'

'Well, I've been doing a lot of thinking. I'm going to have to get a different job.'

'Well, what would you do, though? You'd never hack it in a factory with loads of people, being stuck in one place; what about if you start thinking about everything again? You know, with your anxiety?'

'I've been making a few enquiries. I've been offered a few shifts as a porter in the hospital on the bank with the hospital agency, subject to references.'

'What? You've joined an agency?' asked Audrey, sounding delighted.

'Yeah, asked Stacks to do me a reference for the building and one of the other blokes I used to work with to say I'm alright.'

'That's a really good idea,' said Audrey, becoming breathless. 'I do worry about you, you know, with your back, you won't be able to do that job forever.'

'Once they get all the stuff back, they said to see if I like it first, then they'll put me forwards for a permanent one if a position comes up. Anyway, I need to go and see our Lisa tonight to do that. She said she'd fill it in for me, it's all online… it's double-dutch to me.'

Dave stroked Audrey's head as she flopped down into the chair.

'Brilliant!'

'Are you going to be OK? I hate you being ill.'

Audrey was almost gasping, after just saying a few words. Dave couldn't bear to see her like this.

'No, I'm fine, don't worry about me. You need to go and get your stuff sorted with Lisa. I'll ring you if I need you.'

Dave walked to his eldest daughter Lisa's flat through "the park" - a large stretch of wasteland with a path and a stream. Although there was a children's park at the later end, for the most part the area was largely deserted and unkempt. Filled with shopping trolleys, rubble and other waste, to the untrained eye it was difficult to tell that the stream was a stream. The majority of the area was covered in overgrown trees and bushes. The path that ran next to the stream teemed with undesirable waste; broken glass, used needles, dog dirt and other rubbish. Apparently it used to be a nice area before the train station had become a victim of Dr Beeching's cull and the estate had been built. There was always talk of the park being regenerated and re-opening the station, but this had never happened. Now the trains simply rumbled through the vast expanse of wasteland to the station in the centre of town. After dark, the park was a no-go area for anyone living on the estate, mainly due to the people that frequented the dimly-lit path next to the derelict station. It was only mid-afternoon and not quite dark enough to be threatening. Dave stuck to the path, dodging the pot holes. He vaguely remembered the council making a half-arsed attempt to fill them in not long after they had moved there; now they were worse than they had been back then.

As he walked, he continued to feel panicked about Audrey. He sucked hard on his roll up as he thought about her. *Should he go out and leave her? Would she still be there when he got home? What if it wasn't a cold? What if she had something more serious?*

Some of the drug addicts congregated half asleep on the path, taking their spice. He bid the more alert ones a polite "hello" and continued past. Lots of people were scared of them, Dave wasn't. He realised that he'd been a hair's breadth away from living their lifestyle. He recognised some of them from when he was younger; they had been through the care system. How Ken had never ended living like this was beyond him. Of the ones that he did know, behind their missing teeth, sallow skin and pin-prick pupils, there wasn't one of them that didn't have a horror story to tell. They were people, just like everyone else. The difference was, they had no ability or resources to cope with life. Nobody watched their backs. Forgetting, immersing themselves in chemical alteration of their brains with only each other for company, that was their sanctuary. If he had it on him, he often handed the ones that he knew a few quid or bought them a sandwich when he passed them begging in town. Their lives were hard enough. Dave hadn't spoken to Ken for a week or so. He had tried ringing him, but there had been no reply. In his turmoil over Audrey not being well, he had forgotten about him today.

'Scuse me, guys, anyone seen our Ken? Ken Williams?'

'No, sorry, mate.'

'Not since last week.'

'OK, cheers'

Dave would try again tomorrow to wish him a Happy Christmas.

He reached the stairwell of the block of flats where his daughter Lisa lived. Some dodgy things happened in that area of the estate and he wished that she could move. The call buttons at the front had been smashed in – again. Dave rang her mobile and she let him in. He walked through the entrance and the familiar stench of urine hit his nose. In addition to the usual remnants at the bottom, there was also another foul, putrid smell. In the dim artificial light in the hallway, Dave could make out that one of the flats downstairs had left their bin bags full of rubbish outside. The whole hallway smelled worse than before. He held his breath and started to ascend the stairs. A strong smell of weed wafted down towards him.

As he got three floors up to Lisa's corridor, Dave looked out over the estate. This was the highest point. He could see the homogenous tops of the nearby houses; it looked grim. As he reached the top and walked through her door, he stepped aside for the girl who lived in Lisa's corridor to pass him. Her name was Jade. She had lots of visitors – usually men – at all different times of the day and night. She was thin, too thin, with drawn eyes and a few teeth missing and the remnants beginning to brown. Her appearance was probably not helped by to the stuff that she was sticking in her veins, revealed by the scabs and pockmarks. She looked up at him with inviting eyes and a smile, pausing and waiting for him to talk to her. He politely said 'Hello,' and walked past. Eventually, he reached Lisa's flat and knocked.

'Hi, Dad'.

'Hiya, love. Jeez, it's grim out there in that corridor.'

Dave had missed Lisa since she had moved out last year since having her baby daughter Stacy. Still he managed to see her often. He babysat for his granddaughter when Lisa was at night school. Thankfully for everyone, she had split up with Stacy's dad who was a real waste of space. No sooner had he found out that Lisa was pregnant, than he had done one. Dave was secretly thankful – he was good for nothing anyway. Recently he had been contacting her again, trying to come back into her life. But Lisa was having none of it. She kept herself to herself in the building and so far had never had any trouble. She didn't go out much after dark unless she had to and Dave always made sure that either he, or Audrey and Emma, his other daughter, walked her back.

'Come in, I'll make you a brew.'

Stacy was fast asleep on the rug. Dave handed Lisa the presents that Audrey had wrapped for them for Lisa to put under the tree.

'She's just gone to sleep. Tired herself out playing.'

'Your mum's too ill to come. Her chest is terrible. God knows what's wrong with her; the doc keeps sayin' she's got a virus! But she's had antibiotics now and she's still no better. I've been worried sick.'

'I'm sure it's nothing too bad, if she's on antibiotics they'll kick in soon,' said Lisa reassuringly. She knew that Dave didn't get anxious often, but when he did it caused him severe stress. 'Now calm down.'

'OK, love. I'll have to nip out for a few fags tonight though.'

Dave scooped Stacy up and kissed her on the forehead. She stirred slightly and he wrapped her up in her blanket.

'Shall I put her in her bed?'

'Yes, please, Dad, just don't wake her, she's been awake all day. I need her to sleep tonight. You want her to wake up, don't you? You want to see her.'

Dave just smiled knowingly and stared at Stacy lovingly as he put her in her little bed and tucked her up.

Dave felt proud of Lisa. At twenty-five, she was coping well with being a first-time mum. She was clever too. She was doing an A-level at night school, and she planned on going to college after she had finished it.

'OK, Dad, your CV. I've tried to put as much as I can on it, have a look through it. We'll send it off and see how it goes, yeah?'

'OK, love, I'll have a look at it now.'

They went through it all. Lisa typed it up on her computer and sent if off. Dave read what she had written, it all sounded good. He didn't quite understand technology, it was all a mystery to him.

'I dunno how you do it all, Lis, I don't get these computer things!'

Lisa made another cup of tea and brought out a packet of biscuits, and they sat chatting. She typed away and he wrapped some of Stacy's Christmas presents for her. Usually, he would stay longer. But he didn't want to tonight; he wanted to go home to Audrey to make sure that she was OK. Lisa and Stacy were supposed to be coming to their house for Christmas dinner. But Dave was beginning to worry that Audrey would never be able to cope with making dinner and having people round.

Tuesday December 24th 2020

'Dave… Dave... it's my chest, Dave! I can't breathe, I really can't! It's… it's… got worse!'

Dave put the light on and looked at Audrey lying next to him. She looked pale and her lips had turned a dark blue.

'Right, enough's enough; I'm ringing an ambulance.'

It didn't take too long to arrive. By then, Audrey's whole face looked grey. She could hardly speak. Quickly Dave packed her a bag and accompanied her into the ambulance. The paramedics said that she had a high temperature and low sats. Dave didn't know what that meant; they said it was something to do with low oxygen levels in her blood. He began to panic even more. He could feel the anxiety rise up in his chest, making him feel nauseous, overwhelming him like a tidal wave.

As it was Christmas Eve, the hospital was relatively quiet and they got taken straight into A&E, to an area called "resus". A doctor started taking blood and sticking needles in Audrey's arm and wrist. By now she was more settled, with an oxygen mask on. Dave stroked her head as she lay there.

'We're going to take her up to HDU,' a doctor said to Dave.

'What's HDU?'

'It's the high dependency unit. It looks from the chest x-ray that she's got pneumonia. She's having antibiotics through the veins which are stronger than taking them by mouth, but she's not well. Once we get them in through the tube in her arm, she should get a lot better. I'm hoping she'll be a lot better in twenty-four hours. The best thing that you can do is go home, get some sleep and let us take care of her'.

Tears began to spill down Dave's face. If he was honest, he hadn't really understood what the doctor had said. He had hoped that if she went to hospital and got checked over, they might say that she was OK. But now, they were talking about keeping her in. What if something happened to her?

'No, I can't leave her, not yet. I'll just come up with her for a bit.'

The doctor nodded. 'Look, we'll look after her, we'll do our best, but you need to be there for her too; go and get some rest, her temperature's come down since she's come in, she's better than she was now she's got a bit of oxygen, it all just needs time to work… OK?'

Dave nodded. He put his head in his hands. This couldn't be happening, not to his Audrey. He stayed for a bit longer, just to see her settled. She still looked ill, but she looked peaceful and comfortable.

Christmas Eve had turned to Christmas Day. Dave hadn't registered any of it. He couldn't remember walking out of the hospital. He couldn't remember walking home. It was pitch black outside and he had lost all track of time. He flicked the kettle on and lit up a cigarette. As he stood outside the house he inhaled the smoke deeply, Dave began to worry about Audrey's chest. He always smoked outside, but what if she had inhaled his smoke and got lung cancer? What if it was all his fault? Maybe he should give up. His body began to jitter at the very thought of it, it was the one thing that he knew he couldn't do. *Stop it, Dave. Stop it, Dave!* He looked at his phone - it was 5:45 a.m. Audrey was supposed to have been cooking a turkey, and dinner. Then he remembered, Lisa and Stacy were coming round. How could he even think about cooking a turkey when Audrey was in hospital? Tears began to drip down his face. Then again, no, she would kill him if they wasted it! Dave prepped the turkey, wrapped it in foil, and threw it into the oven.

On autopilot, he began to peel the potatoes, carrots and parsnips to cook them for later – anything to keep busy. The last thing that he felt like doing was eating them. But the girls would be coming round regardless. It got to 9:00 a.m. As he waited for things to cook so that he could cover it all up and put it into the oven, Dave paced up and down the house, going outside very ten minutes for a smoke, thinking, musing, unsettled, not knowing what to do. Eventually, Emma got up. She had been out the night before, returning at her usual ungodly hour of the morning and missed the events of yesterday evening. She wandered down the stairs in her dressing gown, her head still woozy from the night before.

'Mornin', Dad, aw, flick the kettle on. I need a coffee; my head hurts. You're up early. What's wrong?'

'It's your mum, I took her to hospital last night in an ambulance. She couldn't breathe. They've kept her in.'

Emma's bloodshot eyes widened. 'What? To hospital, hospital? Like emergency and all that?'

Dave nodded.

'Well, why didn't you wake me up? Or phone me? How is she now?'

'Stable, they said.' He put the knife down and began to cry.

'Why didn't you tell me?'

'I dunno, love, my head's mashed! I'm just hopin' she's gonna be OK.'

Emma put her arms around him. Then she phoned the hospital to speak to the staff. Audrey was stable and her oxygen levels had increased. Shortly after, Lisa wandered in with Stacy, looking worried and flustered.

'Well, everyone, I can't say I'm hungry, but I've cooked it anyway. We can't go in and see her yet anyway, she'll kill us if we waste it, so tuck in,' said Dave as he poured himself a large glass of red wine. 'By heck, do I need this.'

Everyone sat around in silence as they ate their dinner, pushing most of it around the plate with their forks. No one felt hungry, except Stacy who gobbled hers down. After dinner, they walked into town to the hospital to see Audrey. It was heart-breaking to see her sedated with tubes coming out of her mouth. She was awake but tired; she couldn't say much but she grabbed everyone's hands. At least she seemed more alert. Her oxygen levels and temperature had stabilised.

The next day they had some better news; Audrey has been moved from the high dependency unit to a normal ward. Gradually, over the next week, she improved until she was let out on New Year's Eve. They had had a rather quiet Christmas that year. Dave didn't care, he had his Audrey back and that was all that mattered.

This was both the best and the worst Christmas ever. But 2020 would be a better year all round, right?

Tuesday January 7th 2020

Audrey was still not well. She was short of breath and complained of not being able to smell or taste much. With Christmas, Audrey not working and most of Dave's building work being cancelled due to the weather and frost, they had had little money coming in. But a few days later Dave had some good news.

'Well, Aud, I've got a job, you're lookin' at one of the new hospital porters!' he said. 'Bank for now, but I've got an interview for a permanent job soon.'

Audrey smiled with relief.

'That's great. I have been worrying about what we're gonna do, and how we're gonna manage. I really don't think I can go back yet!'

'Don't worry, just let me look after us for a bit. We can just stay in, not go anywhere, not buy anything big for a bit, and we'll be fine. I've got my savings. We don't need anything, just each other.' He kissed her on the cheek.

'No, you've done enough, I feel useless sitting here. I'll get the ironing done in a minute.'

Emma hugged her mum tightly as she walked into the house.

'Mum, sit down! Let us look after you for a bit like you've looked after us for all these years!'

Dave beamed at her proudly. 'We kept it all ticking along just fine when you weren't here. Anyway, now you're home safe, I'm going to go up to the park and see if anyone has seen our Ken hanging around. I've been trying to phone him all over Christmas, but it just goes to answerphone. I've heard nothing. I went to his last address and he got booted out for not paying his rent the week before Christmas'.

'Oh God, I hope he's OK,' said Audrey. 'It's been freezing out there this last week!'

'I know.'

'Well has Elle heard off him?'

'Nothing.'

If anyone knew where Ken was, it was usually his daughter Elle. But this time, even she didn't have a clue where her dad had gone.

Dave wandered up to the park. He had been that preoccupied with Audrey being unwell that he hadn't really thought about the fact that he hadn't seen or heard from Ken for a few weeks. The first person that he came across was one of the working girls, Anita.

'Hi, Dave, love, you looking for some fun? Audrey finally kicked you out?'

'No, Anita, I'm not here for that,' replied Dave, laughing. 'I just want to know if anyone's seen our Ken?'

Anita shook her head. 'No, not for a few weeks. He came up here, and scored off one of the lads about a week before Christmas, but I haven't seen him since.'

It turned out that nobody had seen Ken. Dave had walked around town, been to his brother's last address and been to the addresses that some of the people who he hung round with lived. Finally, he checked the homeless shelter – nothing. They decided that it was time to report him missing to the police. Elle rang them.

Disheartened, Dave headed off home. He had to be in work tomorrow on the building site and it was going to be a cold one. Still, only two weeks to go and then he would start in the warmth, doing something worthwhile, helping people and keeping active. Now that Audrey was a bit better and he had no worries, Dave was looking forward to a new challenge.

He racked his brains about where Ken could have gone. He often went underground and disappeared for a couple of weeks, then he would pop up somewhere. Usually he would have had a spell in hospital, or he would be in jail, or would have moved to the other end of the country for a month or two, having met someone with an equally chaotic lifestyle, sofa surfing and living on the streets. Ken's life was so erratic that Dave had difficulty in keeping up with him. He wasn't on social media and Dave had lost count of how many mobile phones he had lost. But after a week or so, he would always let him know where he was. Not this time – this was the longest that Ken had ever gone without telling Dave where he was. Dave was beginning to have the old recurring nightmares about finding Ken dead in a ditch somewhere.

Because of his drug use, they had had to stop him coming round to the house when the girls were little because he was often off his face. Audrey had complained of money going missing out of her purse. Even though Dave loved Ken dearly, he just couldn't trust him around his family. They did what they could to look after Elle, who often came round to play with the girls. But not Ken - the possibility that he might ruin Dave's haven, his sanctuary, by tainting everything that they had worked hard for was just too much. Dave's house was nothing special, in fact it was basic. But it was his.

Dave racked his brains for where else he could search for Ken, but he drew no conclusions. He would just have to re-trace his steps the next day.

Thursday January 30th 2020

Dave took a deep breath as he left the house. The cold crisp air filled his lungs and he started the mile and a half walk to the hospital. He was to have an induction session today before starting work.

Although she was much better than she had been, Audrey was still not right. She planned to have another two weeks off and then go back to work the week after next. Despite what had happened over Christmas, Dave still felt optimistic. He was worried about starting something new as he found change difficult to deal with. But he knew that he had to do it. He couldn't work on building sites much longer, it was a young man's game. Besides, with his back going into spasm every time he challenged it, what good was he to anyone? Maybe he would hate it in the hospital and have to find something else. But he would give it a go.

The induction session was an eye opener. It was nice to sit in a nice warm seat and be paid to learn interesting things. Topics included health and safety, trust policy and safeguarding patients and children. It was a bit like being back in school, except for the fact that he was enjoying it! He learned about manual handling and some other important issues like dealing with difficult patients and how to use the computers. It was all very exciting - he had a new spring in his step.

Dave's first shift was a night shift. He had to shadow another porter, Ajay, a jolly man in his sixties, originally from Pakistan. Dave felt nervous about having to start over again, meeting people. Their first job was to move a body from the respiratory ward to the morgue. Ajay showed him how to put the body in the bag, then onto the trolley and transport it. The patient's name was Mr. Evans and he was eighty-five. Dave felt spiritual wheeling him off on his final journey down the corridor.

'I know it's winter, but by heck I've been up on that ward a lot this year. We never usually have this many dying. I've never seen the morgue so rammed!' said Ajay.

Dave nodded. 'Does it ever, you know, get to you, like?'

Ajay nodded. 'Every time I move a body from the children's ward, which luckily isn't that often, or from upstairs in maternity, I still sob my heart out. And I've been here over twenty years!'

Their next job was to transport Mrs Owen to x-ray. Mrs Owen was a rather cantankerous lady. She didn't smile when they approached the bed.

'Have a go, Dave, and if you need help, let me know,' said Ajay. 'I'll just wait here.'

'Bring that bloody chair closer to me, 'ow do you think I'm gonna get in there?' The nurse rolled her eyes as Mrs Owen complained away.

'Yes, ma'am, of course, ma'am, is this close enough for you?' asked Dave, bringing the chair closer. The nurse and Ajay began to stifle giggles.

'No.'

'Well, if I bring it any closer, ma'am, I fear that I'll ram your legs. Is it that you can't walk the ten centimetres or so to the wheelchair? Is it that you need assistance?'

'Yes! You can walk can't you, Marian? And I think that that chair is more than close enough!'

Mrs Owen shot the nurse an evil look, tutted and got into the chair. Dave began to wheel her off.

'Can't you slow down? You're goin' too fast.'

'No, I'm afraid not, ma'am,' replied Dave. 'Your appointment is in five minutes and we'll miss it if I walk any slower; you don't want to stay here any longer, do you?'

Mrs Owens tutted. Dave wheeled her into the x-ray department.

'Right, I'll be back to pick you up when you're ready.'

'What? You just going to leave me here? Aren't you going to stay with me?'

'No.'

'Well, I never.'

'See you later then.'

'Well done,' said Ajay. 'You handled that very well. Most patients are nice, but you always get the occasional miserable arse who complains about everything and anything!'

Just as they went to walk off, the bleep went. Dave answered it. It was to transport a patient to the rehabilitation ward. Then the bleep went off again, it was a call from x-ray. By now, Dave had taken a few patients and essential items to and from the wards. The bleep was getting a bit more frequent.

'Look, Ajay, I'll go to A&E, I'll be fine; I'll give you a shout if I need help.'

'OK, we'll meet back up after I've been to x-ray.'

Dave walked down to A&E. So far he was enjoying his job. Seeing people, helping people, and it was all nice and warm in the hospital. He was met there by the nurse.

'Mr. Williams, fifty, alcoholic hepatitis, needs to go to ward nine.'

'OK, ta, sister.'

Dave picked up the notes, placed them underneath the wheelchair and went to collect his patient. He opened the curtains. There was Ken.

'Ken! I've been tryin' to bloody phone you for the last four weeks! Where the heck have you been?'

'I've been bad, Dave! I got chucked out the gaff, went back on it, now I keep throwin' up, blood an' everything!'

Dave pulled the curtain around them and walked over to Ken. He put his arms around him and hugged him tightly. Dave had never ever seen his brother looking so unwell. His skin was grey, his eyes were yellow, his legs and abdomen were more swollen than usual. He was dishevelled and unwashed, and looked like he had been for some time.

'Why the bloody hell didn't you phone me? You know where I live? Why didn't you tell me?'

Ken shrugged. 'Dunno mate, I'm too far gone, aren't I? Who wants to see me like this? I know I'm ill! But I just can't stop, Dave!'

'Well, Christ, Ken, I don't care what you look like, I'd have tried to help you! Let's get you to the ward, and get you right!'

Dave helped Ken into the wheelchair and took him up to the ward.

'Aw, Ken, again,' said the sister on the ward. 'Hi, Ken, God, he looks ill this time though!' she said quietly to Dave.

'That's my brother actually. Look after him, won't you? He's not had the nicest life, neither of us did.'

The sister looked at Ken, and then looked at Dave. 'No way! Jeez! I won't ask what happened.'

Dave nodded. 'I know. Can I give you my number? You know, just in case he needs anythin'?'

Dave gave the sister his number. She promised him that she'd take good care of his brother. Dave breathed a huge sigh of relief. Now at least he knew where Ken was.

At the end of his shift, Dave nipped back up to the ward to take Ken some Lucozade and toiletries that he had bought him from the hospital shop. He was unable to stay as it was dinner time. Reassured that Ken was comfortable and settled, Dave walked out of the hospital and back down the road towards home.

It was fair to say that he had enjoyed his first shift. It was drizzling, but that was nothing compared to working outside all day on a building site and getting soaked. Dave pulled his hood up; it was just over a mile and a half home.

His thoughts turned back to Ken. In the next street, he passed the old building where he and Ken had once lived in the squat. It had been turned into a trendy block of flats with the old Victorian features restored. Dave sighed as he remembered back to those days. How far he had come since then, how happy he was, how grateful for what he had. But life had not been as kind to Ken. With every year that passed Dave wondered whether or not Ken would make it to Christmas. He wondered about the other people who had stayed there and he had not seen since - what had happened to them? Were they still alive? Dave hoped that they too had found peace. He couldn't think about it all for too long, it brought back bad memories. Then he started feeling guilty again about Ken. He thought about his parents, about his mum, neglecting them when they needed her the most. And his dad; how could he do that to her? *Stop thinking about it all, you'll drive yourself mad!*

Life was unfair. But Dave reckoned that the most important thing was to learn from experience. From the moment that his girls had been born, he swore that he would never leave them, never neglect them, never not tend to their needs. But for now, with the knowledge that Ken was at least in a place of safety, Dave would go home and have a sleep ready for tomorrow night. Besides, Audrey was making a chicken dinner later, and her chicken dinners were the best!

Friday February 7th 2020

The bleep went off. It was to move a body to the morgue. It was the bleep for the job that nobody ever wanted to do - a bleep to go to the children's ward. Dave and Ajay walked slowly in silence down the corridor with the stretcher. They rang the bell and walked in; the staff looked solemn.

'It's an expected one. This is a fourteen-year old boy called Archie, found hanging in foster care...'

In foster care! In foster care! In foster care! The words rang in Dave's ears like tinnitus. Then they got into his head, and swirled around, and around, and around. Before he knew it, his eyes had welled up. The nurse glanced up at him, and stopped talking.

'Are you OK?'

Dave nodded his head and wiped his eyes.

'Yeah.'

'Look, we've all had a good cry over this one. Palliative care for suspected brain death from being found hanging, intubated, but he passed away once the tube was taken out.'

This kid could have been him, or Ken, or any of the others who were in care. What had that poor lad been through to make him want to do that? How many of the others who had been brought up there had done that? Please god, say that being in care hadn't made him do it, please say that the system had changed! Dave couldn't bear to think about it. Tears poured faster his face. He fought hard to stifle the sobs. The nurse handed him a tissue.

'Are you sure you're OK?'

Dave nodded again.

'Yeah, it's just, I was in care when I was young. It was horrible. I remember a few kids that, you know, couldn't cope.'

Ajay put his hand on Dave's shoulder. 'Dave, you wouldn't be human if you didn't care. My heart is breaking for this lad as well.'

The nurse pulled the curtain around the bed. Dave looked down at the boy. He looked just like any other young lad, sleeping, with his short brown hair, and a slight smile across his lips. His face looked peaceful. Dave hoped that he truly was at peace. Questions raced through his mind. How had the boy ended up there? Who did he live with? What was it that had tipped him over the edge? Were they kind to him?

'Sleep tight,' Dave said as he touched the boy's face. Ajay began to zip the bag up and they arranged it on the trolley.

'Take a minute. Sit down. I'll fetch you a cup of tea,' said the nurse.

'That would be lovely. One sugar for both of us please, if you like, Dave?'

'I'd love a cup of tea, and to just sit down for a bit.'

He put his head in his hands. 'Sorry, mate, I'll pull myself together in a minute.'

'I didn't realise that you'd had it so tough, Dave.'

Dave drew in a deep breath.

'Yeah. Apart from the eight years I lived with my nan until she died, me and my brother had a horrible childhood. I try not to think about it. My brother Ken, he takes drugs, you know, to forget about it. But this, seeing this lad, just, you know, brings it back.'

'I feel for you, my friend, but you are a brave man, braver than you realise.'

The nurse returned with two cups of tea for Dave and Ajay.

'Thanks,' said Dave.

'No problem. We could all do with a break and a cup of tea after that.'

'Sorry. I pitch up here, blabbering like a baby, and you lot have had to watch him die. You must think I'm a right dipstick!'

She shook her head.

'We do get these horrible ones occasionally. Not very often, but we do get them.'

Dave and Ajay drank their tea as they sat, thinking about the boy.

'God, he must have hated his life to do that!'

'I know, he must have not been able to see any other way out!'

'But at least here he passed surrounded by a lot of love and care,' said the nurse.

Dave put his hand on the trolley.

'Well, young man, did you hear that? You did matter, you were loved. By all of us. Now we're going to take you for your final ride, me and Ajay here.'

Dave and Ajay finished their tea.

'Are you sure you're OK, Dave? I can do it myself if you want.'

'No, I want to help him.'

'Ready?'

'Let's do it.'

They wheeled the trolley up the hospital corridor to the mortuary entrance. They wheeled Archie through the door. Ajay paused as they entered the corridor just before the chapel.

'Dave, my religion is different to yours, but I don't think that matters. Shall we pray to God for this lad?'

Dave nodded. 'It doesn't matter who to, Ajay, in here, in our hearts,' he said as he pointed to his chest, 'we're all the same; let's just pray to a God, who will look after him.'

Dave and Ajay bent over the trolley, shut their eyes and prayed to God via their own respective religions. Each had only one simple request – peace for the young boy in front of them. Once they had finished, they took the body through the doors of the mortuary.

'Are you sure you're gonna be OK? Why don't you ask to go home early? I can cope for the next half an hour, it's gone five, it'll be quiet now.'

'No, thanks, Ajay, thanks for offering, but I honestly think that I'm OK. You see, even though he's passed, I'm helping him. That feels nice. Those people that used to be round me, in the homes and that, they weren't there to help. I am. And that's the difference.'

Ajay smiled up at him and put his hand on his shoulder.

'Besides, if I leave you, you'll have a rush on or something.'

The porter's bleep went off.

'I'll get it, Dave, if there's another one, take it, if not, chill for a bit.'

Dave didn't get another bleep. He walked home with the young boy not far from his thoughts. Walking his usual route he passed the old squat. Once again, he started ruminating. It wasn't doing him any good. Instead, he turned his thoughts to what Audrey was making him for tea. Fish stew tonight – Dave always felt happy after eating one of Audrey's fish stews! Dave decided that from now on, he would take a slightly longer walk home down a different street.

Under the confidentiality agreements, he wasn't allowed to tell anyone what he had seen in work. But when he got home, Audrey could tell that there was something wrong with him.

'What's up?' she asked.

'I've just taken, well, someone to the morgue, that's all. It was just a bit upsetting.'

'Oh no. I did worry about you, you know, seeing things like that!'

Dave shook his head.

'It was from the children's ward, Aud, it was horrible for Ajay too and he's been there years.'

Audrey looked up at him. She didn't say anything.

'Funny thing is, I don't feel anxious. I feel almost as if, in a funny way, I helped him as best as I could. It's just, it could have been me, or our Ken lying there, you know, when we were that age. It's got me thinking back again. I need to stop doin' it! Me and Ajay even ended up prayin' for him as we took him back.'

'Look,' said Audrey, 'are you sure that this job is for you? Are you sure that it's what you want to do? What about, I don't know, something that's not as emotional, like being a security guard, or working in a shop, or…'

Dave shook his head.

'No, Aud, it's not that. I like the job, I really do. It's just, stuff like that, I'd be upset if I hadn't been, you know, brought up where I was.'

Two weeks later, a small funeral service was held for the young boy in a nearby church. Amongst the mourners were Dave, Ajay and some of the staff from the children's ward. They had barely known him, but he mattered to them.

Saturday February 22nd 2020

People in the hospital were getting twitchy. There was a lot of talk about coronavirus, a new virus from China, apparently. They said that it had originated in the wet markets, but people had their suspicions.

Symptoms included a high temperature, bad cough, tight throat and inability to breathe, all of which could lead to pneumonia. They said that there was no cure except supportive treatment which meant going on a ventilator. When Dave thought back, he was convinced that that was what Audrey had had – she'd had all of those symptoms and hadn't even improved when she took antibiotics for pneumonia.

This week she had gone back to work. Audrey complained that she had never been able to taste anything properly since being ill. She said that she was happy because she'd lost some weight and looked good. Dave always thought that she looked lovely anyway and secretly thought that she had lost a bit too much weight, but he dared not pass comment.

Ajay often commented that they seemed to be shifting a lot more bodies than usual to the mortuary, with many dying of unexplained causes. But as Dave had not been in the job for as long as Ajay, he had no idea what was normal and what wasn't.

Luckily, Dave was able to visit Ken every day in hospital. They said that his liver was failing because of the drugs, alcohol and his generally chaotic lifestyle. In the past, Ken had caught hepatitis from injecting drugs which had caused further damage. He needed intensive treatment and fluid drained from his body. But whenever he went into hospital, he had very few viable veins left to place any cannulas so it always took ages. That evening, Dave popped onto the ward before he started his shift. Ken was sitting up in bed, looking miserable.

'Alright, mate? What's up?'

Ken huffed. 'I'm fed up. I'm fed up of all this,' he said, holding his arms out. 'I just feel like it's time for me to go.'

Dave pulled up a chair and pulled the curtains around them.

'Aw, mate, come on. You're not dead and buried, you've got a life to live. You've had enough of it taken, start living!'

'Yeah, but you're happy, with Audrey and the girls, it's like they're your heroin! I tried it, with Karen, and even when we had Elle, it just wasn't enough for me, I just couldn't forget and move on! It's like I can't be happy, I dunno how to be, I can't cope with normal things!'

'Well, Elle's worried sick about you, you know?'

'I'm full of guilt, Ken, I feel bad that I didn't sort myself out, then you could have moved in with me instead of going in that home. Nothin' can ever make me forget, or move on! I'm always looking for something else, something to numb the pain. Every time I try to get off it, or go straight, I end up just going back on it to make me stop thinkin' about it again. I might as well not be here, I'm livin' half a life!'

'Look, Ken, I know what happened to us when we were young, it was bad! But Nan loved us, it wasn't all bad! Don't ever feel bad about me! And now, since I've been living on me own, I've had a brilliant life! But nothing's going to change for you until you stop doing what you're doing. You can't start to get better until then! Look at yourself, you're yellow! Elle's grown up now, she doesn't need you like that anymore, she just needs you here.'

'I know, Dave, I just can't stop though! The consultant came round today; he told me the only hope I've got is having a liver transplant'.

'Jeez, Ken, is it that bad? You've wrecked your liver?'

Ken nodded. 'Yeah, it's had it!'

Dave put his head down.

'That's why I'm full of fluid, and yellow. I'm slowly dying, Dave! I know I have to stop, but I can't do it! They said they'll never give me a liver transplant while I'm still wrecking it.'

Sometimes Dave was amazed that Ken was still alive after everything he'd put his body through over the last few years. And in all honesty who could blame the doctors for denying Ken a liver? Dave didn't know much about transplants, but surely it would be better to give a liver to someone who was capable of looking after it.

Deep down inside, Dave knew that Ken was dying, a slow, painful, protracted death. The Ken that he had known as a child had died inside many years ago; all that remained was this battered shell of someone that Dave barely knew anymore. He loved his brother, but Dave knew that Ken's life was nothing but a living hell on earth. Nothing could help him. Without his drugs and alcohol, Ken couldn't cope being forced to live in reality. The same reality that he had spent the last thirty years or so trying to escape. Dave sometimes wished that it had been him who had found their mum, or spent more time in the home; maybe he'd have coped better? Maybe Ken would have had half a chance? The more ill that Ken became, the more hatred Dave carried for the ghosts of the past.

Suddenly, the curtain was ripped from around them.

'Time to go now, sorry, visiting's over.'

'OK, I'm just leaving.' Dave handed Ken some Lucozade and grapes. 'Right, see you tomorrow, pal.'

As he turned to walk into the main corridor, Dave passed one of the healthcare assistants. He had met her a couple of times. Short, she had a face that looked as if she was constantly chewing a wasp, almost as if her personality correlated perfectly with her face and expressions. She was always offhand and very rude.

'Who's this for?' she asked the nurse in charge as she took a tray with food on it as Dave walked out of the bay.

'Mr. Williams in bed eight.'

'Aw, the druggie with the buggered liver?'

Dave shook his head as he walked past. That was his brother that she was talking about. OK, he might be a "druggie". He did take drugs. But he took drugs because his life had been so traumatic that he couldn't do without them. He took drugs because he could not function, living with the pain of the past. Before he knew it, he had turned on his heels and was heading back towards the morose creature walking towards Ken's bed with his dinner.

'Excuse me, can I have a word please?'

She turned and huffed at him.

‘Can’t you see, I’m very busy at the moment, can’t it wait?’

‘In private, please,’

‘Well, can’t you just say whatever it is to me here?’ Dave had his porter’s uniform on, he looked as if he was working. She probably had no comprehension that he was there visiting as opposed to working.

‘OK, well, seeing as you’re happy, I’ll say what it is that I want to say to you here then, shall I?’

‘Yeah, yeah, whatever, if you must.’

‘OK, well that “druggie” that you’re referring to in there, that’s my brother! Not ideal to take drugs is it? We all know that. But if you found your mum stabbed to death on the floor by your dad when you were eight years old, got passed around from pillar to post and ended up in a kids’ home round here, where, let’s face it, we all know what happened, you’d probably take drugs to forget as well.’

‘Well, I…’

‘It’s a bit like, just like you put make up on to hide the fact that you’re ugly, not only inside, but outside as well, he takes drugs to cover all that up. So don’t let me hear you talking about him like that again; you’re here to look after him, not to judge him!’ Dave walked off.

‘I think your staff here needs some training on how to address patients, calling patients “a druggie” isn’t very pc these days is it? Nor is breaching patient confidentiality and telling the whole ward what conditions he’s got either?’ he said to the nurse in charge as he walked past her with her mouth dropped open.

Dave felt very glad that he had just done his induction training and sounded as if he knew what he was talking about.

Monday March 2nd 2020

It was a miserable March morning. Dave had just finished nights. He had one more shift and was looking forwards to a rest for a few days. First, he had to look after Stacy for an hour while Lisa handed in her final piece of coursework at college. Dave met her at the bottom of the flats just outside the entrance. She was excited as she now only had one more exam to do in June. She handed Stacy and the buggy to Dave. He planned to take her to the supermarket and the park before going back to the flat while they waited for Lisa. Dave didn't like going to that park. It was rough and sometimes covered in litter and drug paraphernalia. But Stacy liked going on the little swing.

'In case the swing is covered in crap, the wipes are under the buggy,' said Lisa.

'No problem, love, see you in an hour or so.'

At every opportunity, they made sure that Stacy got the chance to play outside, and see trees, and flowers, and do cooking with him and Aud. Dave often visited the charity shop on the estate and bought her books and toys. Dave didn't enjoy reading but he found that he could read the ones written for her easily. He dreamed of a better life for her, a life away, far away from this part of the estate. He just knew that one day, Lisa would make it. For now, he supported her as best as he could.

Dave and Stacy strolled around the aisles of the supermarket. It was 8.30 a.m. on a Monday morning. Audrey - ever frugal - had realised that things were reduced to half price at this time on a Monday after the weekend. Dave often popped in when he finished his night shift on the way home and got some goodies. He stood there browsing in the reduced section, feeling extremely uneasy, not knowing why.

'Look, Stacy, it's your favourite! Melon!' he said, picking up a half-price gala melon.

As he continued to wander around he couldn't shake off the strange, creepy feeling. Unease. It was worse than anxiety, it was a feeling that he hadn't experienced for many years. But why? He racked his brains. He came to the conclusion that he had nothing to be stressed about! Dave re-played it all again in his head; Audrey was better, he had a new job, alright, he earned a bit less than he had before, but there were always the extra shifts and they weren't excessive spenders! What else was worrying him? The girls were OK, Ken was being placed in sheltered accommodation and was no longer homeless, there was all this talk of coronavirus, but even that hadn't really bothered him. Everyone and everything else was fine! What was the matter?

It was starting to do his head in now. He had been OK for a good few weeks, apart from the odd blip. But suddenly, for some reason, it had come flooding back over him like a tidal wave! But why? He started to question everything. The unease that he felt was more than anxiety - almost as if it was an actual threat as opposed to a perceived threat, as if someone was watching him. Like when he was in the home and his social worker left him there, or when Blackwell beckoned him to come into the woodshed, or when he lay in bed at night fearing that he would be taken. *Come on, Dave, you're being ridiculous!* He looked around: there was no one there.

He got half way down the next aisle to the dairy section. For the life of him, Dave couldn't remember what it was that he was supposed to buy. Then he heard a cough, a deep, throaty, hacking cough: the type of cough that comes from lungs damaged beyond any salvage that belong to a thirty-plus a day smoker. He could smell smoke, and something else; a strange, familiar waft of Lambert and Butler cigarettes – the ones he'd never been able to stand the smell of since - mixed with sweat and grease, a smell that made his stomach turn. Dave turned around slowly. He knew exactly why he had been feeling anxious; he had dreaded this moment for over thirty years!

Leslie Blackwell stared at Stacy as he half-limped, half-walked towards her. The now horrific wrinkled skin was set deeper, his greasy black hair greying but the same unkempt style, the smell, the unwashed, greasy, oily stench mixed with body fluids followed him. The aisle seemed to be closing in, the lights in the shop were brighter, the floor moving towards the ceiling. For a few moments, Dave's body paralyzed. Blackwell limped closer, fixated entirely on Stacy. Dave had always said to himself that if he saw him again, he'd have a massive go at him, then knock him out, or break his good leg, but all that he wanted to do was run, to get out of there as fast as he could.

'Awww, ain't you sweet!' He smiled at Stacy. His brown teeth were now rotted away to blackened uneven pegs. Stacy looked up at him and began to cry.

Dave turned his back to him, unclipped Stacy and grabbed her out of the buggy to comfort her, burying his face in hers. His instinct was telling him to run, far away, so that Blackwell couldn't say anything, or do anything to hurt her, or even look at her, but something else was happening, anger was welling up inside him, like a huge volcano for which there was no outlet! Dave was here, right in the middle of the supermarket! He put the melon down, clasped Stacy tightly to him, pushed the buggy and began to walk away out of the shop. Leslie Blackwell, fixated on Stacy, hadn't noticed him, he was sure of that.

Ever since he had seen him in the pub all those years ago, he knew that he still lived somewhere in town. But this? After being convicted as a paedophile, coming back here was brazen. How did the guy have the guts to walk around the shop? Unless people didn't know him?

Dave shut his eyes as he got out of the shop. There it was; the office, the bedroom, the showers, the garden room. He could feel his head being smashed into the radiator, the belt swinging down towards him! He opened his eyes. He had to get himself together – he had Stacy with him! He had to sort himself out! Quickly!

He left the shop and sped around to the nearby park. On autopilot he wiped the swing down, not even noticing if it was dirty. Then he stood, pushing Stacy on the swing, watching the entrance to the supermarket. Anxiety washed over him like a tidal wave as he again began to remember. He felt as if he was fifteen again, as if he was in care, at the mercy of Blackwell and Evans. But time had moved on, and so had Blackwell's age and capabilities. *Come on Dave, pull yourself together, what the hell is he gonna do to you now?*

'Grandad, melon?' said Stacy. His hands shook as he pushed her on the swing, eyes fixed on the entrance to the shop opposite as he sucked hard on his roll up. Dave tried his best not to smoke around Stacy, he hated himself for doing it, but he needed a fag. Eventually, the limping figure emerged from the door.

'Don't worry, babe, I'll get you your melon. But first, we're going for a little walk!'

'No! Melon, Grandad, now!'

Stacy began to cry. Dave fished around in his pocket. He couldn't have her kicking off if he was going to follow that slime-ball and see where he was going - they needed to remain inconspicuous. He found a small packet of biscuits that he'd robbed from the hospital induction day and handed them to her. Lisa would kill him if she found out, but needs must.

As she munched contentedly on her biscuits, Dave took Stacy out of the swing, strapped her into her buggy and pushed her down the road, following the limping figure in front of him. He kept as much distance as feasibly possible between them. Blackwell looked so frail, so evil, yet so pathetic. Like a character from a horror movie for children, that wasn't quite frightening enough to scare an adult. Although once you knew anything about Leslie Blackwell's history, he was every bit as frightening as a character from a Stephen King novel. He limped on towards the main road. Just before he reached the end, he stopped to chat to a woman with a little boy. Dave began to feel nauseated at the sight. Did he know that little boy? Did he have regular contact with him? Did the lady think that he was a "nice man"? To avoid catching up to him, Dave slowed his pace and pretended to look for something underneath the buggy. Blackwell eventually limped off towards the top of the road.

The woman with the child continued towards them up the road. As she drew level with Dave and Stacy, he stopped her as she passed him.

'Excuse me, love, that bloke you were just talking to, I'd give him a wide berth if I were you with, your little boy; he's not a very nice man as far as kids are concerned, if you know what I mean!'

Blackwell had nearly reached the top of the road. Dave hurried off with Stacy, leaving the poor lady with her mouth hanging wide open. Blackwell turned right onto the main road. Dave and Stacy got to the end just in time to see him turn down a side road into a cul-de-sac where the sheltered accommodation bungalows were. He pushed Stacy slowly along the road, watching as Blackwell opened the door of one of the bungalows and hobbled in. It was just around the corner from where Ken's new flat was going to be. Number seven! Lucky for Dave – now he knew exactly where he lived! This gave Dave an unexpected degree of comfort; an odd sensation having spent all those years avoiding him,

He turned around and walked back to the supermarket in a daze, mulling it all over. A large grin spread across his face as he realised that a power imbalance had just occurred.

He went back into the supermarket and picked up the melon, luckily it was still there, now the price had been reduced even further! This really was Dave's lucky day! As he wandered around the shop, preoccupied, he couldn't quite remember what else it was that he was supposed to buy, it was something about bread, milk and pasta – yes, that was it, Audrey was making tuna bake for tea. He paid for his groceries at the till, placed them in a carrier bag and left the shop.

After, he walked back to the park with Stacy and pushed her on the swing for a bit longer, ruminating over the events of the last half an hour as he did so. He felt unusually happy, and the grin remained fixed across his face for the remainder of the morning. He carried Stacy, the bag of groceries and the buggy up the stairs to the flats. He didn't even notice how heavy or light it all was, or that his back was aching. All he could think about was Leslie Blackwell. Once at Lisa's flat, he put Stacy down, and cut the melon up to give her a piece. She was happy. She fetched him a book and he read it. Half an hour later, Lisa returned.

'Thanks for looking after her, Dad. Hope she's been OK.'

'We've had a fantastic morning, love! Bloody great!' He kissed Lisa on the cheek and picked Stacy up for a cuddle.

After he had stayed for a cup of tea with Lisa, he walked back home. Not through the park, but down towards the main road and past the cul-de-sac where he had just seen Leslie Blackwell go. Purely out of morbid fascination. No longer threatening, a mere limping old man on a stick, vulnerable. Did he have any family? Had he got married? Did he have anyone who looked out for him? Dave doubted that anyone so evil could cope with a family, at least not a normal, functioning one. He stopped and looked down into the road to where Blackwell's bungalow was. Feeling compelled to walk down there, hammer the door down and lay his hands on that filthy animal, it was all that he could do to stop himself.

'They've got me, Dave… I can't forget what happened…'

Ken's words rang in Dave's ears again, and again, and again.

A hornets' nest had been stirred. Something that he had never felt before bubbled up in Dave as his mind reached a strange kind of equilibrium; as if he had felt afraid for no reason for the past thirty plus years, as if it had all been a lie. But it hadn't, had it?

It was thanks to people like Blackwell and Evans that Ken was in the mess that he was. No longer afraid, Dave needed revenge. But not today. He had to think. Eventually, Dave forced his legs in the direction of home, because most of all, he needed some sleep before his shift that night.

Audrey had gone to work and Emma was at teacher training college. He put the kettle on, made himself a strong cup of coffee and rolled a cigarette. He sat in the lounge, smoking roll up after roll up. Ruminating. Drinking endless cups of coffee. Soon he would need to go to bed, he had to be back up for six. Feeling nauseated at the prospect of eating anything, Dave skipped the toast that he usually made when he got in from work.

He usually slept soundly in the day when he worked nights. Under normal circumstances, he would be in bed by now. Today, this was not going to happen. He craved a shower – to rid himself of the slight smell of sweat and grease. He got into the shower; the warm water bounced off him and made him feel better, if only for a while. He scrubbed his skin, again, and again, and again.

He got into bed, but he couldn't sleep. Every time he shut his eyes, there was Blackwell's face, Evans's face... their evil eyes bearing down on him. He wanted to see them, to cause them pain, to make them too afraid to look at him. After a few hours, he eventually drifted off for what seemed like a couple of minutes. Shattered, it was time for him to get back up and go to work.

Up he got. With his eyes red and dry, Dave got ready and trudged back to work through the small piles of snow that had fallen during the day. Agitated, preoccupied, ruminating. Luckily, it was a week night which was quieter than a weekend night. The smells on the wards, the dirty linen he had to transport, cigarette smoke on his lunchbreak, the distinct remnants of Lambert and Butlers as he walked in and out of the smoking shelter, too many times tonight. He had to. His adrenaline heightened, he jumped every time his bleep went off, or someone shouted, or even spoke to him. He had to get out of there! But he couldn't – he had only just started! He was on his trial period. If he just upped and left, he'd get the sack for sure!

By the time that his shift had finished, Dave was shattered – utterly shattered. The last time that he had felt that tired in work was when he had spent the night on the streets of town behind the swimming baths after he had run away from the care home. He felt as if he would drop on his feet. Luckily it was his last shift; now he had five days off. Five days when he could just stay in, and try and calm down so that he could think rationally – that was what he really needed to do.

Thursday March 5th 2020

Dave sat alone in the living room. He smoked the roll up and let it burn right down to the brown stain on his finger. Eventually, it began to burn into his skin. He didn't notice or feel anything as it singed the tips of his fingers.

He sat there, alone in the room, flicking aimlessly through the TV channels. Replays of old Man City matches were on. Dave usually watched them. But he couldn't concentrate. His brain was racing, preoccupied. He had thought that it was bad when he used to have anxiety, but this was something else, this was 10,000 times worse than that! The compulsion to go round to Blackwell's bungalow with a box of matches and a petrol-soaked rag, or a knife, or a spade to finish off his other leg, it was all too much; thoughts intruded into his mind against his will.

When he mused it over, he should be laughing at Blackwell, he was an old man with a limp. Limping around the streets with a stick! A couple of years perhaps off needing a Motability scooter? All thanks to him, Dave Williams. What was he going to do to Dave now? What could he do? Dave could leather him any day! But the fact was, he was still out there, he was there! There was no getting away from him! Dave longed to hear him scream again. For him to feel pain – unlimited amounts of pain! Pain that never ended – just like they had tried to inflict on him and the other kids, the kids whose lives they had ruined, like Ken's.

Everyone knew that there was something wrong. Audrey kept asking him if he was OK. Ping - another text from her. He ignored it. Lisa kept phoning him. Emma was off today and kept making him cups of coffee and things to eat that he left as he couldn't face them. He sat smoking in the lounge. Dave never usually smoked in the house like he had for the past few days, not since before they had had the girls. He detested the thought of smoke round his girls and now Audrey. He didn't care. Nobody had even confronted him about it, they were all just worried about him. He had stopped picking his phone up. He couldn't face carrying on, telling them over and over again that he'd be OK. They all knew that he wasn't.

He was supposed to be working back in the hospital the next day – on day shifts. He hadn't slept all night with the worry about the prospect of having to go to work.

Crippled with anger and rage, what if someone annoyed him and he decked them? He would lose his job for sure. He didn't think that he could go in; he wasn't capable of doing anything except sitting in the house, hidden away from society that needed protection from him should anyone rile him. He ruminated over it all again and again and again, chain smoking his roll ups. Here he was, safe, cocooned in his house. Safe with his family and his girls. All he ever wanted was to be happy, and he was happy when he felt safe, where he could stay, and just see everyone that he cared about the most. It was safer to stay in the house, in the chair. Hidden away from the world, where he couldn't bump into Blackwell or Evans, the reminders of the hell on earth, the terrible memories, his conjecture about what had happened to Ken. About his nan, the other homes, his mum, the other lads, *make it stop!*

He shuddered as he remembered the other bad things from way back when; the feeling of the cold damp frosty air with the frost glistening on the inside of the window of the house with no heat; he shut his eyes as he remembered the cries from his mum as his dad hit her around the house followed by the silence which was worse. He remembered how he had woken up that night and she wasn't there, how she kept going out, leaving them on their own when they moved to the new house. Then she'd come home, with money for herself to buy alcohol, but nothing for them. She had left them, freezing, sitting in squalor. He shut his eyes tightly, and just like that, there he was, he was six years old again. He put his hands over his ears and closed his eyes to make it all stop, but it wouldn't.

He thought about his girls, how he would die for either one of them! Or Stacy! Or Elle! Why had nobody ever felt like that about him or Ken? Nobody except for his nan? Tears began to drip down his face as he thought about her; she'd know what to do. But he had no one who knew him, Dave, from when he was little. No one who cared about him the way he cared about everyone else, or ever had except for his nan. Not the people who had been paid to look after them, the ones that just sent them away when they got a bit too much, to worse places, places where kids got ripped out of bed in the middle of the night, or watched in the shower, or beaten. It was a bitter pill to swallow, it was so unfair. *Make it all stop, like it did when he felt happy!* Or had it ever? Really? It was always there, stuck at the back of his mind.

He looked up to his mantelpiece, at her picture. The one he loved the most, the one that Audrey had paid a lot of money to have enlarged and re-done for Christmas one year. There she was, looking down at him, with her kindly face. His nana! Dave was nine, Ken was ten. She was cuddling them on the beach. She had taken them to a caravan for their holidays. And then he remembered the good times again. Dave stopped crying as he remembered the promise that he'd made to her. This was no good, none of this was doing him any good!

But then it only took the smallest of things to remember. As he tried to stop thinking about it, Dave felt hungry, he realised that he hadn't eaten all day. Then he remembered the feeling of pain in his tummy when he wasn't given enough to eat! *Aargh, someone make it stop!* He shut his eyes tightly, trying to forget it all, but it was no good.

He tried to concentrate on thinking about what he had, living in the house that he and Audrey had proudly purchased from the council, their girls, his little piece of heaven on earth. To other people, that might be seen as failure, as someone who hadn't done much with their life. But Dave felt like a millionaire! As if he had won the lottery several thousand times over! Here, he was safe, with his family, with his girls, they were all more precious than gold to him. He had been marooned, on his safe little island with them. Until now, until that scumbag Blackwell had reminded him of how it used to be.

'Dad, I'm off out now, do you need anything?' asked Emma.

Dave couldn't think whether he needed anything or not.

He shook his head. 'No, love, I'm OK, ta.'

'Are you sure you're going to be OK, Dad?'

Dave forced a smile at her. 'I'm fine, love. Don't worry about me.'

'Dad, you know you can talk to me, if you want to...'

'No, it's fine love; it's better left alone.'

Emma stood looking at him for a few seconds; he could tell that she was contemplating whether or not to leave him just yet.

'Em, I'm fine. I'll be OK...'

'I've got to go to work, I don't want to leave you like this; you're not... going to do anything stupid are you? Not like Uncle Ken does?'

Dave shook his head. No. Not that, he had too much to live for... he would never do that!

'No, love, I promise, OK? I'd never do that, not to you lot.'

'OK. Well, if you want to talk to me, just text me and I'll come home.'

Shortly after the front door had clicked shut, Dave emptied the last bit of his tobacco from out of the packet into the roll up, but there was hardly any in there! He had no more left. He felt his chest paralyze with fear. He needed more – he couldn't cope without it at the moment. There was no one who could go to the shop for him. He jumped up out of the chair and ran to the front door; Emma had disappeared down the street. He tried to phone her; he heard a buzzing on the mantelpiece, she had left her phone there. Audrey hadn't finished work. He had no idea when Emma would be back or where she had gone. He was in a mess, he would be in an even bigger mess without his tobacco. He would be climbing the walls by the time she got back. It was no good, he couldn't do without a fag; he would have to go out, he had to!

Tears welled up in his eyes as he shuddered at the thought of leaving the house. Slowly he rose from the chair, shaking with trepidation about what he would do if he saw or had to speak to anyone that he knew. Dave felt pathetic, so pathetic - he couldn't even go to the shop! But he needed another fag! He had gone through three packets of tobacco already today. Usually he smoked not even a quarter of one in a day. Wanting to remain inconspicuous, he pulled on his black hooded top, scarf, and gloves and set off to the shop on the estate. It was chilly outside. Just chilly enough to excuse being dressed in this attire - surely nobody would recognise him? There were people milling around in the street. He pulled his scarf up high around his mouth. He couldn't face making small talk to anyone, not today.

The day was fading into dusk. The park was fast becoming a no-go area with the fading light - what should he do? The unappealing option of walking through the park felt a hell of a lot safer than the alternative of walking down the main street and having to see people and talk to them. As he contemplated where to go, his legs turned left all by themselves. The more he thought about it, the more the park seemed like a better option than the street; he would rather risk getting beaten up and robbed than having to interact with others. Besides, it was still too early for most of them to be out. And cold.

As he went through the gates and into the wasteland, everything swirled around and around in his head. Walking through the park in the final dim remnants of the dusky evening, he noticed someone walking in front of him up ahead. He walked slower, not wanting to catch them up, just in case it was someone that he knew. He couldn't face talking to them, he just couldn't. But then he noticed something else; the person walking in front of him was limping, and leaning on a stick.

Dave hung back.

He was approaching the bowels of the park, the overgrown, rubbish-strewn, rat-infested part where the working girls and the rent boys congregated. This was where some of the kids hung round taking drugs and stuff. The man stopped and turned to the side, then carried on limping off down the path. Dave stopped as he realised something. There was only one reason that a fella who was as old as that would venture out at this time of night: he was waiting for them – the vulnerable people of the night! The man started walking again and stopped under the light of one of the only remaining lamp posts which had not been smashed.

He should have known from the limp! It was him! Leslie Blackwell! Sharking around to find those who he could use to fulfil his disgusting lustful fantasies. Now he would find it difficult to force himself on anyone, therefore he needed the services of the vulnerable, the exploited, those who had fallen into the mire.

Anger welled up inside him; his blood began to boil as his whole body became incandescent. Dave felt his legs automatically began to stride faster towards the limping figure in the distance as it continued to amble slowly across the park, watching and waiting, unaware that he wasn't the only predator there! Dave scanned the area; there was definitely no one else around – just him and Leslie Blackwell!

He double checked again as Blackwell walked into the part of the park with the now derelict station where the working girls and boys took their clients, by the overgrown and unkempt shrubbery. He checked all around the park again, and again, and again. No one coming, no one going, no one waiting for anyone at the sides of the path: not yet. Dave could just about make out some of the waste and vandalised items around him; a few bricks, rubbish, slate tiles and a long piece of metal from a smashed up concrete bollard, rusty, with spiky bits pointing out. Perfect! Dave pulled his scarf up higher to cover the lower part of his face and pulled his hood down further over his forehead leaving just his eyes visible. He picked the metal bar up. It was heavy, heavier than he expected it to be, but that didn't deter him. He moved slowly and stealthily, creeping closer to the limping figure.

A freight train rumbled towards the park on the adjacent railway line just across the stream. As the noise dimmed out the snaps of branches and rubbish underfoot, Dave sped up until he was directly behind Blackwell.

As he reached him, he swung the metal bar as hard as he could into his back. Leslie Blackwell let out a blood-curdling cry as he buckled and fell forwards, writhing in agony. Dave stood, waiting.

'Stop, please, I beg you, p… please don't hurt me!' he whimpered as he rolled over onto his back, cowering, his legs tucked into his chest. Dave paused for a few moments, lulling Blackwell into a false sense of security. Gradually, the man straightened his good leg out to prop himself up.

'What do you want? Money? I've got money!'

Dave began to laugh, a slight snigger at first, which slowly built up into a rapturous crescendo.

'Yeah, I'll get you money now…'

Blackwell was shaking with fear underneath him. Dave didn't want his filthy money. As the man fished around in his pocket for his wallet Dave swung the metal bar again, straight into Blackwell's left shin, not once but twice, just to make sure. His laugh was hollow as he heard the crack, even above the noise of the passing freight train. Blackwell screamed in agony and tried to pull both of his legs up into his chest. He stood watching for a few seconds, enjoying the sight of Blackwell squirming in agony below him.

'Aaargh, aaargh!'

Dave swung the bar up over his head for a fourth time, with the full intention of slamming it down into the side of Blackwell's head to finish him off once and for all. But as he held it above his head with both hands, he stopped. He would kill him for sure – what if he got caught? There would be a full murder inquiry. What if he got sent to prison? Lost his job? What if Audrey and the girls couldn't manage? If he couldn't see them, it would kill him.

As the freight train rumbled off, Dave scanned the area, satisfied that there was still no one around. He threw the metal bar into the cess-pit by the side of the stream, turned on his heels, and disappeared into the undergrowth, leaving Leslie Blackwell incapacitated, writhing around in agony. Eventually, he came to the wooded path that ran around the perimeter. No one in their right mind would walk around there at dusk. Blackwell's screams grew louder as the freight train rumbled off. As Dave walked quickly down the path, the screams soon became inaudible.

Dave scaled the old brick wall that separated the park from the alleyway leading to the back of his house and walked swiftly down the path behind, checking again – no one was around. If nobody had seen him, he could never have been there! He crept into the house via the back door and took off his gloves, scarf and hooded top. He opened the washing machine and threw them straight in on a high wash. Then he sank back down into the chair in the living room. As he did so, he began to laugh, louder, and louder, and louder. He contemplated what must have gone through Blackwell's mind as Dave swung the metal bar into his back; he laughed as he thought about how loudly the man had screamed; he laughed louder as he remembered the sound of the crack of Blackwell's left shin bone as it shattered under the weight of the metal bar. As he thought back, the terrible memories that he had been forced to think about for the last few days seemed to fade into obscurity. Dave felt good, really good; no longer agitated, or possessed, or vengeful, just content, for the first time in many years, as if the memories of the past that he had fought so hard to suppress for all this time somehow didn't exist anymore.

Dave doubted that in the bitter dark March wind and rain many people would venture across the park unless necessary. Poor old Leslie Blackwell would have to stay there. Even if someone did find him, until an ambulance came he would have to lie in the wretched chill for the next half an hour or so. Dave hoped that it would rain and soak the frosty ground so that when someone eventually found him, half-dead, or at least, wishing that he was, it would be too late to do anything much with his leg. He reached to his side for his tobacco – he would make a cigarette to celebrate. Then he remembered, he remembered exactly why he had gone out in the first place. He needed a fag, not anywhere near as much as he had needed one before, but he still needed one.

The door clicked; it was Audrey, back early from her mum and dad's.

'Hiya love, you OK? I need some baccy, I've just run out!' he said.

She had just taken off her coat, she looked chilled to the bone, her face wind-chapped and bare of make-up, her tousled hair that she had taken out of her hairnet and not had chance to brush, falling down in waves. She still looked beautiful; God, he loved her. He would be no one without her.

'OK, I'll just nip back out and...'

Dave got up from the chair as she reached back onto the peg to put her coat back on, presuming that Dave was in no fit state to venture out to get his own tobacco.

'Aw, don't worry, love, I'll go myself, you're frozen.' Dave kissed her on the cheek.

'Are... are you feeling better?'

'I am. Much better. He pulled her in close to him and kissed her on the lips. 'See you in a bit.'

Dave opened the back door and virtually skipped off to the shop leaving an astounded Audrey staring after him, wondering what on earth had happened to him, and why his anxiety had disappeared. One thing was for sure, he would be taking the long way around, down the main street to the shops, past all the CCTV cameras.

Dave remembered that he needed to act normally, but that was hard. He grinned to himself as he walked down the street. He couldn't stop thinking about the look on Blackwell's face as he had smashed the axe into his right shin all those years ago, and he remembered how much he had enjoyed repeating the same exercise tonight.

There was a CCTV camera situated on the lamppost in the street, there were a few people mulling around. Dave noticed his mate Neil walking up the road towards him.

He stopped right underneath the camera pretending to tie his shoe laces. He hadn't seen Neil since he had left the building site.

'Alright, Neil, mate? How's it goin?'

'Alright, Dave, mate!'

They stopped and chatted for a few minutes. Dave reckoned that should there be any need by anyone to question his movements, he would feature prominently standing in the street talking to Neil in the footage. Then he would be able to claim that he had gone to the shop down the main street to buy tobacco and not through the park. Besides, it was nice to see Neil. They said their goodbyes and promised each other that they would meet up for a drink down the pub the next time that Man City were playing.

Dave realised that he had made partial peace with his past. There was only one tiny regret that Dave had – how he wished that he could have finished Blackwell off! Well, if it didn't happen this time, there was always the future, and the future was bright. He, Dave, would enjoy life more from now on. Maybe one day to top it all off he would even get to learn about the whereabouts of Reginald Evans. He rubbed his hands together in glee as he strode off down the road.

Audrey had planned to make Dave an appointment to see his GP the next day to discuss his anxiety. He had never spoken to anyone about it before and really didn't want to. Talking about it just took effort, and dragged things up. And that night, he slept for ten hours straight. He went back to work the next day with a spring in his step.

Wednesday 11th March 2020

Over the next few weeks, the word on everyone's lips was "coronavirus". People were getting scared. There were no confirmed cases in the hospital yet, but they hadn't started testing anyone. The Welsh Assembly Government had announced that they would be setting up a test system in the next few weeks. Dave was fed up with receiving emails regarding the matter. He had gone from getting around five a day, to over fifty, all full of big words and concepts, some of which he failed to understand. Then just as he had got his head around the changes to be implemented and he thought that he understood it, it all changed again. Dave was confused; so were the other porters.

'I'm so sick of all these messages!' he said to Ajay.

'Yeah, me too, I can't face reading anymore! But I'll probably miss the most important one and get the sack if I don't!'

'I know. I feel like that; it's only the threat of gettin' the sack that makes me carry on looking, to be honest!'

'Imagine having two weeks off, and coming back to all these!'

'Or being sick for a month! And having to wade through all this! It seems like it's changing every hour!'

'Well, it sounds to me like we're not alone! It sounds like no one knows what we're supposed to be doing! Even people above us! One minute we don't need masks and gloves and aprons, then the next we do but they can't get them. It's like the whole country doesn't know what to do, the whole world, in fact!'

Dave's bleep went off. It was children's ward. Then Ajay's bleep went off. Then Dave's bleep went off for a second time. It was A&E.

'Here we go, Ajay. I hope it's not that horrible nurse on today, the one that's dead rude, I'm not in the mood for her.'

Dave went and picked a little girl up from x-ray to transport back to the children's ward. As he entered A&E, the snapping sister was there waiting.

‘When I bleep, I expect you to come!’

‘Yeah, so does everyone else, love!’ replied Dave. ‘Anyway, what’s making your patient more important than the seriously ill kid I’ve just wheeled off from x-ray who they bleeped me about first?’

‘Well! I’ve a good mind to put a report in for you about being so rude,’

‘I’m asking you a serious question here…’

The snapping sister in A&E was a monumental bully. Nobody liked her. When challenged, she threatened to report people. Dave had had several altercations with her. As far as he was aware, no reports had ever been made about him.

‘Anyway, I’m glad you’ve got time to, love, coz most of the time, I don’t even get time to go to the loo, never mind bugger about on the computer with trivia!’

One of the hospital cleaners was scrubbing around the bays. She stifled giggles as she mopped away, as did one of the doctors sitting writing at the computer station. Noticing, the sister seemed to become even angrier.

‘Mrs Thomas, bay two,’ she snapped as she stormed off.

‘Of course I will, sister, right away, sister, immediately.’

But today, even the snapping sister couldn’t bother Dave. This was his last shift for a few days. Everyone reckoned that there was a lockdown coming and things were shutting down. After recent events, Dave had decided to seize the moment and make the best of the time that was left. It was his and Audrey’s anniversary soon, thirty years since they had had their first date! If there was a lockdown coming, and no one could go out anywhere, they were going to have a good one even if it meant celebrating early.

Audrey had booked a couple of days off work. Dave had asked her to pack a bag because he was taking her somewhere special. She was excited. He dared not tell her where or how much it was costing because they had just started getting back on their feet with money. Audrey would not want to know. But Dave could afford it. Plus, there was overtime going at the moment as droves of staff seemed to be going off sick.

Early the next morning, they caught the train from town. Dave had booked a hotel for the night in a picturesque town a few stops down the train line. It used to be a tourist place in years gone by. It was one of Dave's favourite places. It retained the quaint Victorian streets and shops. Even in the winter, baskets of seasonal flowers adorned the walls of the shops and houses. There was no litter to be seen anywhere. People were polite, if somewhat posh compared to what Dave was used to. He had gone there on a day trip with his nan when he was little. She had taken him and Ken to a little sweet shop just up the hill by the train station. Audrey had been before; they used to take the girls to the same shop when they were little, but they hadn't been back for a few years. He was dying to know if the sweet shop was still there so that he could fetch them some back; strawberry bonbons for Lisa, rhubarb custards for Emma and Ken. Dave became excited as he imagined what he would buy for Stacy.

Audrey had dyed her hair and got dressed up. She looked lovely, even lovelier than usual. Dave carried their bag and led her by the hand as they walked into town to the train station. They boarded the train and sat watching the sites as it sped down the track into the countryside. Dave sat back and relaxed. So many of the sites on the line were still the same from when he was a child and he grinned, feeling all nostalgic as he remembered back to the good times that he had had with Ken and his nan.

The train sped towards the centre of the town. The stop was coming up; Dave stood up to get his case down.

'Aw, I love it here!' said Audrey. Dave winked at her.

It was too early to check-in. They took their bags to the hotel and left them in the safe. They meandered around the quaint cobbled streets and had some lunch in a "brasserie". It was all very posh. They did some shopping, found the little sweet shop to get the girls some sweets, then checked in and put their walking boots on. They headed off on a lovely walk that followed the river, taking them into the countryside just outside the town.

They had a posh dinner, retired to bed, and drifted off to sleep in each other's arms.

The next morning, they ate their breakfast and, after wandering around some more shops, took the train back just after lunchtime. Dave had taken a copy of the morning paper from the hotel to read on the train. There were only the posh ones left, a different read to his usual paper. The one that he usually read had free coupons for caravan parks, girls dressed in bikinis, and other stuff. But this one was different, more factual, with a few big words here and there that he didn't understand. Undeterred, Dave carried on. Eventually, he came to the news section. There was a piece on coronavirus.

'They reckon we're heading for a lockdown, Aud, they're already having one in Italy and other places. Apparently the virus is rampant there, and they reckon we're only two weeks behind them.'

Audrey looked up from her magazine.

'I think I've already had it, Dave. What else could I have had? It must have been that!'

Dave nodded. 'I know, love, it must have been.'

'It'll spread about, won't it? Think about how many people we've been around this weekend? How many places we've been? How many people have coughed or sneezed round us?'

'I know, and if there's a lockdown coming, this might be the last chance we get to go anywhere for a while. So I hope you enjoyed it.'

Audrey nodded at him. 'I'd enjoy going anywhere with you, and I'm not going to ask how much you spent.'

Dave sat back and looked over at her, contented and serene as usual, reading her magazine. He smiled to himself. If there was a lockdown coming, there was no one else that he would rather spend it with. Whatever happened over the next few weeks or months wouldn't matter. And still, nobody had come asking him any questions about Leslie Blackwell. Dave wondered if they ever would.

Friday 13th March 2020

Dave walked into the supermarket and was greeted with a surreal and unbelievable sight, people with trolleys piled high with food and toilet roll. Jeez? Toilet roll? As far as anyone was aware, this virus had nothing to do with the toilet. Dave felt that to be fair, if anyone had had such trouble with their bowels or they needed to use that much toilet paper, they should have been to the doctors long before this outbreak happened! People were beginning to panic. He had only come for a few things. Audrey was making a tuna pasta bake tonight and he had to get pasta and a packet of paracetamol for Emma's hangover. She had been out with her college mates for one last time and had a bad head.

Dave made his way round the shop. People skulked past him, some having to hold the tops of their trolleys so that the shopping piled high didn't fall off. Jeez, it was as if an apocalypse was coming! Dave put a few things in his basket. Eventually, he reached the shelf where the pasta usually was. It was empty. He double checked that he was in the right place – yes, there were the prices, but the shelves were nearly empty. The only pasta left was a weird green colour. It was dearer than the pasta he usually bought too. Made with spinach, it looked horrible, but it would have to do. He picked it up and continued around the supermarket. The shelves were looking bare in many of the sections. There was lots of stock left in the deals section in the middle, camping stuff and clothes. And the sun cream bit was full.

Dave came to the medicine section next and looked for paracetamol - none anywhere. The shelf was empty! They said that if you had the virus, you had to take paracetamol to reduce your temperature – maybe that was why? Shaking his head, he picked up a packet of ibuprofen and two of the last bottles of kids' paracetamol instead.

As he walked around, he began to worry. What if there were food shortages? What if they had nothing to eat for a bit? Dave put a few things in his basket that they didn't really need but might be useful should a crisis occur; packets of noodles, frozen chips, tins of soup.

Dave had far bigger worries today. He was off the next time that Man City were playing. He had planned to go and watch the match in the social club down the road. But it had been bloody cancelled! Now Dave felt extremely depressed about this – what would he do if he couldn't watch his beloved team play? When would the games be reinstated? Out of all the problems that COVID-19 was causing, this was by far the biggest one.

Oh well, they said it would all blow over in a few weeks and things would get back to normal. But from what had been happening around the rest of the world, Dave wasn't too sure.

Thursday March 19th 2020

Dave and Ajay had been called to a meeting in work with the other porters. It was all about the virus. It turned out that some people had to start doing something called "shielding". Shielding involved staying in the house and not going out. It sounded absolutely horrific. It was mostly for the over-seventies and people with specific health problems. None of them were over seventy. But some of them had health problems.

After the meeting, Dave was talking to Jimmy. Jimmy was one of the older porters and he had something wrong with his lungs from smoking, which was something to do with reduced lung capacity and he couldn't breathe very well. Shielding meant that he could no longer be in work until it was safe. He looked relieved when he realised that he would need to be furloughed which meant staying off work on eighty per cent pay. Dave looked over at Jimmy; he smiled as if he had just won the lottery.

'Brilliant, that's ace! It's like superdole, innit?' he said to Jimmy, who smiled and nodded.

Ajay had asthma and used inhalers. This meant that he was at high risk. Dave watched the look on his face as he realised that he too might have to go off work. Ajay lived with his wife and three kids in town. He was immensely proud of his kids. His eldest daughter had just finished university and his son was going to train as a pharmacist next year. As he had done for his daughter, Ajay planned to support his son through university by doing as many extra shifts as he could. He was a proper hardworking, family man. He was a good person who desperately wanted to work to help his family. In contrast to Jimmy, Ajay's face dropped when faced with the possibility of being furloughed.

'You OK, mate?'

'Well, I'm a bit worried to be honest, Dave. If I have to go off, I couldn't do any extra shifts to help my son. You know, when he goes to uni?'

'Well, you never know, you might not have to, just coz you've got asthma. I bet loads of people have it; surely not everyone is gonna have to shield?'

'Well, I hope not, and flaming hell, I'm gonna be bored stiff at home! Stuck with the missus in the house all day long! I don't know if I can hack it!'

As it turned out, Ajay didn't have to shield. His asthma didn't fit the criteria for shielding. He was ecstatic to still be in work.

Over the next week, things started closing down. Pubs shut, clubs and restaurants shut. Ajay complained that he couldn't get his hair cut because the barbers by him had shut. It was as if the whole world was slowly sinking into an abyss.

'Brill, just think mate, with everyone off, an' the hospital bein' so busy, there'll be a pile of overtime goin'!'

'That's the only good thing about this whole mess, Dave.'

Monday 23rd March 2020

There was an announcement from the prime minister

'You must stay at home.'

The next minute, the phone rang. It was Lisa.

'Dad? Does this mean we won't be able to see you for the next god knows how long?'

'No. I don't think you can, love, unless it's people you live with.' There was a long pause. 'Which you can do if you want to? You and Stacy will have to share the little room mind…'

There was another long pause. 'Dad, can we? I really don't think that I can't see you and Mum. I don't think I can cope being on my own in that flat. Even if it is just for a week or two.'

'Well, of course you can, me and your mum would love to have you back here, wouldn't we, Aud?'

A big smile spread across Audrey's face. They missed Lisa dreadfully. It just hadn't been the same since she'd gone. It always felt like one of their arms or legs had dropped off, as if their family was somehow incomplete. Emma missed her too. Stacy could be hard work at times, but for the most part it was lovely to have a little one around. At least they had a back garden here; as unkempt as it was at the present time, it was somewhere for her to play. Plus they had easy access to the hills and mountains from where they lived.

'OK, well, that's sorted then. Pack some bags and we'll come over and help you carry them, won't we, Aud?' Audrey nodded enthusiastically.

Audrey and Dave walked to Lisa's down streets which were unusually quiet. There was no one hanging around outside the pubs because most of them had shut. There were no kids hanging around on the benches at the entrance to the "park", there were barely any cars driving around. Everything had just - stopped.

Eventually they reached Lisa's flat and found a sharp contrast to the rest of the world.

Cars pulled into the car park, kids sat around on the benches outside, dogs ran freely around the streets. Lisa opened the door for them and they made their way up the stairs. People sat on the stairs chatting. On the top floor, Jade, the young lady with the rotting teeth who frequented the stairwell, was still in business. Undoubtedly she would continue to receive visitors. Here, in the flats, it was as if nothing was happening outside of the building, as if the flats and the entirety of their occupants were oblivious to the impending pandemic. Dave and Audrey felt relieved that Lisa and Stacy were coming with them.

'What if they all notice us moving her stuff out and rob the place?' whispered Audrey.

'Well, there's nothing we can do, except not leave any of her decent stuff behind.'

'Hi, Mum and Dad.' Lisa had begun to pack some of her things away. She had already prepared two large wash bags and a wheeled case. Stacy was asleep in her pushchair.

'Right,' said Dave. 'Our Lisa, you're gonna have to take your most important stuff first. Not being funny, but they're still all outside, hanging round on the stairs and stuff. If they think you're going, they'll be in here. So what's your most expensive or important stuff?'

'Well, I was gonna pack just my phone, some clothes and toiletries. But maybe I should pack the TV and stuff instead?'

'What about your jewellery? Anything you need for college, your laptop and stuff for Stacy? We can always come back again tonight and tomorrow; I'm just thinking long term, you know, if someone breaks in?'

Lisa packed things that she wanted to bring, in order of how much they meant to her as opposed to what she thought that she needed for a couple of nights. She left most of her kitchen items and clothes that she wouldn't wear and they made their way back down the stairs.

'You moving out, love?' asked Jade as she stood aside to let them pass.

'No, just staying at my mum's for a bit so I can finish off my college work.'

Once Stacy had been put to bed at her grandparent's, they left her in Emma's care and went back to Lisa's flat.

Dave booked a taxi. They filled it with whatever furniture they could take apart, her TV and other big items. The other stuff, most of which she had bought second hand anyway, would have to stay there for now. As Dave looked up to the stairwell, he could see a couple of the more dubious occupants of the flat watching them, waiting, as if they were circling around to see what she was fetching and carrying, and if it would be worth their while to go and have a look. They were making Dave extremely annoyed.

'Nothing to see here, we're taking all the good stuff.'

By the time they had returned home it was gone ten o'clock.

'I feel shattered now!' exclaimed Audrey, who had worked all day. 'My thighs are aching from walking up those stairs. I think I'm going to have to go to bed.' Dave kissed her goodnight and he and Lisa had a cup of tea.

'It feels so nice to be home,' said Lisa, sinking back into the chair.

'I bet you're gonna miss living on your own though.'

'I will do, but I'd like to think I'm not going to be there forever, Dad. It's OK for now, but I don't want Stacy being brought up there.'

Dave nodded.

'Some of them people that live there, I hate the thought of you even havin' to walk past them!'

'I know. I just don't know who anyone is apart from Jade. I keep my head down in there and just get on.'

Friday March 27th 2020

Typically, seeing as it was lockdown, the weather outside was glorious.

Dave was enjoying having Lisa and Stacy living with them. In their spare time, the girls planned to weed the back garden. It was a mess. Audrey had always wanted a pergola, and red roses. For a few years no one had bothered with the garden, there always seemed like more important things to do. When Dave had been working on building sites, the last thing he felt like doing when he got home or on his days off was his garden. Now there was a little one in the house, nothing to do and nowhere else to go, it was time to remedy the situation.

Nowhere was open for non-essential supplies. Outside paint, plants and garden materials were not things that were considered to be essential. Dave had to think outside the box; how could he make the outside better without spending any money? The fence needed painting and re-doing where it had fallen down, and there was a tumbledown shed in the corner with a leaking roof. The wood wasn't bad. Dave reckoned that he could use it for something. The grass was high. And the shrubs and plants needed trimming and attending to.

Dave mowed the lawn. He hadn't done it this year and the pleasant spring sunshine had resulted in the grass starting to grow again. The rickety old shed was becoming dangerous, especially with a two-year-old around. He opened the door, cleared the rubbish out and began to dismantle it. Dave kept the wood and decided that he would use it to make a smaller shed with a little den at the back for Stacy to play in.

Clearing the shed he found the old BBQ in the back with some charcoal that had somehow managed to avoid the dripping roof. He began to scrub and clean it. To his dismay, looking round the garden, Dave realised that a great deal of mess had been generated in the process. He also realised something else that was even worse than it had been before. The one thing that Dave had always disliked about the garden was that the whole estate could see right into it. Now that the shed was dismantled, the problem was worse. Maybe if he built Audrey a pergola, they could have some privacy? Dave wondered what to do. Then an idea hit him; why hadn't he thought of it before?

A sunken garden! If they could dig down at least half a metre in the bottom of the garden, no one could see them while they were in it. That would also create some much needed soil for Audrey to do the garden the way that she liked it and privacy for everyone. It would be a lot of work to do, but Dave reckoned that they had more than enough time to do it. He borrowed some spades from Barry and Shelia next door, disinfected them and the girls got on them, digging and digging until they had dug a good half a metre of soil out.

The dustbins weren't due to be collected for another week, there was lots of rubbish from the shed, and bonfires had been banned. Dave stacked the waste up in a neat pile in the corner of the garden and took a couple of carrier bags with him every time he went somewhere. He placed them in bins around the streets. Audrey and Lisa set about trimming the bushes in the garden back and weeding the flower beds.

The garden took little under a week to finish. Once they had dug down, Dave sprinkled some grass seed and used the old slabs from under the shed to make steps going down to it. Standing in the bottom of the new garden, they could have been living anywhere. Nobody could see them, except for Barry and Sheila.

'Do you know, Dad, I'm beginning to enjoy this lockdown business! It's quite fun really!' said Emma as she helped Dave smash up a concrete bollard with a pick axe.

'It is,' grunted Dave as he hacked away at the concrete. 'I've been dying to do this since we bought the house off the council, bloody awful cheap fencing! There, now we can use the rubble to build your mum's flower beds up at the sides!'

That Friday evening they had a BBQ. Stacy flaked out after eating her burger. As they sat there having a drink and listening to music, despite being in lockdown, everyone was happy. Audrey nearly had her flower beds that she had always wanted, the garden was private and the pergolas were planned. Barry and Sheila chatted over the fence and the sun shone down, it was happy days!

Under the new regulations, everyone was allowed to do an hour of exercise every day. The next day was glorious. Audrey made a picnic and they all went for a walk up the hills. As they neared the top, the whole town fanned out in front of them. Standing on the hill, the town and life itself looked smaller, more manageable somehow, like things always did when you looked at them from a different point of view.

'Wow, I haven't been up here for years!' said Emma.

'Na, me neither,' said Lisa. 'I just keep forgetting it's here.'

'This is where me and your mum came on our first date,' said Dave.

They sat and ate their picnic, gazing down over the town.

'It's lovely up here! I'd forgotten how much I love it,' said Audrey.

'Yeah, me too,' said Lisa. 'I don't think I've brought Stacy up here before.'

Dave smiled contentedly. It was stressful at work, but at home, everything was cool. It was almost as if there was no pressure. No pressure to buy things that they could do without anyway, or go to places that they didn't need to go to, or do things that they didn't really want to do. Even better, he was surrounded by his girls. As long as he had his family and they were all safe, lockdown could go on indefinitely.

Wednesday April 15th 2020

During the day, the hospital felt like a building that was in the middle of being decommissioned. Nobody came to clinic in outpatients, A&E was silent, no visitors swarmed the corridors at the allocated times and some of the wards had been temporarily shut with staff re-deployed. Many staff were shielding. Remaining staff had initially worked copious amounts of overtime to compensate. Regardless, nobody wanted to come to hospital for fear of catching COVID.

In contrast, the estate was buzzing with life. Everybody was out and about. Dave had never seen the place so busy. When he and Audrey walked up to the mountains, they bumped into more people from the estate that they knew on that one trip than people that they had seen all year. The weather was extremely fortunate and on the hills, wildflowers were springing up. Trees were covered in blossom and they had found some lovely new walks around and about. While everything else had stopped, nature had carried on.

Ken had moved to a rehabilitation ward in a community hospital. Dave was no longer able to visit his brother. Ken had been allocated a flat in the complex just behind Leslie Blackwell's bungalow that was being renovated and the lockdown meant that progress had been delayed.

Life continued.

Monday 27th April 2020

'Where to?'

'Ward 4X.'

It had been a while since Dave had been up there. It was the orthopaedic ward. Orthopaedics as a whole had been quiet since sporting events had been cancelled, people had stopped travelling far and fast in cars and routine orthopaedic operations such as hip and knee replacements had been cancelled. The staff had been allocated additional duties and some had been redeployed. They were not happy.

'No problem, love, have you got the notes?'

'Yes, they're here in the bag. Just watch his left leg, he's got osteomyelitis in the pins.'

'Osteomyowhat?'

'Aw, sepsis, of the bone in his leg. He was attacked apparently. Had to have his leg pinned and now it's all gone wrong and gone septic.'

'Oh dear me!'

'Also, he's got a cough, we're not sure if he has COVID or not, so don't get too close. And it'll save your nose - apart from not being the most pleasant, he's not the most hygienic!'

Dave had another half an hour until the end of his shift. He had to take this patient to the ward and then he was going home. They had finished a lot of the garden now and he had some grand ideas. Barry and Shelia had given him some cuttings for Audrey to plant, and they were going to have a barbeque later.

Dave pulled back the curtains of the cubicle; he had never felt so glad to be wearing a mask.

'So', said the nurse who had followed him to the bed, 'this is Mr. Greenwell, date of birth sixth of June 1956, just had his leg pinned and we don't think it's quite settled properly so he's back off to the ward.'

There, sitting on the end of the bed with his left leg covered in plaster was Leslie Blackwell!

'Er, just got to go for a sec, love? Look, I'm sorry, but I really need the loo, is that OK? I'll be with you in five, OK?'

The nurse looked at him crossly. Dave retreated into the main corridor as his heart pounded faster and faster! It was him! It was definitely him!

Mr. Greenwell? Was he taking the mick? Dave slipped into the staff toilet to compose himself. Palpitations rose up in his chest and his breathing quickened! Him! It was him! After all this time, he hadn't seen him anywhere for years! Now he had seen him three times in two months! How could that even be possible? He had changed his name. That was interesting. Dave began to laugh, and laugh, again, and again and again. Then again and again and again as he remembered the snapping sound in Blackwell's leg and the piercing screams of agony he made. Dave waited for the anxiety to come back, just like it always did. Nothing!

After a few minutes, Dave composed himself and left the toilet. He pulled his face mask further up past his nose just to make sure that he was as unrecognisable as he could be as he walked back towards the cubicle.

'OK, mate?' he said to Mr. Blackwell. 'Just hop into the chair here.'

'Right, just got to get you out of bed, Mr. Greenwell,' said the nurse.

'Watch my bloody leg!'

'Yes, we will, Mr. Greenwell! If you let us help you, we can get on with our jobs. Now get up like the physio showed you.' Clearly annoyed by "Mr. Greenwell's" attitude, the nurse snapped impatiently. 'Then you can get out of here, can't you?'

Dave got the distinctive impression that the nurse was not particularly enamoured with Blackwell and couldn't wait for him to leave the ward.

'Well, come on then,' she said.

Eventually, following much protesting, Leslie Blackwell got into the wheelchair. The nurse rolled her eyes at Dave and tutted as he wheeled Blackwell away.

'Good luck with that one,' she whispered. Dave simply smiled back at her, then, realising that she couldn't see his mouth, he raised his eyebrows.

His hands felt powerful as he gripped the top of the wheelchair, pushing Blackwell along. Several times, intrusive thoughts regarding how he could cause Blackwell even more pain flooded Dave's mind. He walked Blackwell past a large metal dinner tray cage, but refrained from ramming him into it. Maybe he could catch up to Ajay wheeling another patient up in front and accidentally bump into them? There was always the top of the stairs... As they reached the door of the ward, Dave advised Blackwell to move his leg in out of the way of the door frame. Oh dear, he had swerved a bit too far to the left.

'Aaargh, you bloody idiot!' Blackwell exclaimed in agony as his leg became sandwiched between the door and the frame.

'Sorry, mate, you need to keep your leg in.'

'Well, I bloody can't, can I?'

'The bed's not quite ready yet,' said the nurse. 'We're having to scrub everything down now after every patient and deep clean, we'll be another few minutes if you're OK to wait.'

'OK,' replied Dave. 'Where shall I put him for now?'

'You'll have to wait with him just outside while we scrub the area, sorry.'

'No problem.'

Before they had left the other ward, Blackwell's notes – as usual for patients - were under his chair in a carrier bag.

'Right, wait out here, I'll be back in a moment.' He turned Blackwell around and wheeled him back into the corridor. 'Mind your leg this time…'

The staff toilet was just off the ward. Dave pulled the carrier bag out from underneath the wheelchair. Blackwell, still reeling in pain from bashing his leg on the side of the wall, didn't notice. Dave headed off to the toilet.

'Just going to the loo, mate.'

'Christ, you like going to the loo, you, don't you?' Blackwell said sarcastically.

He locked himself in the toilet and started reading. He turned to the first page. “Name: Leslie Greenwell. 7 Connor Close.”

A small smile crept across his face.

The A&E notes for this admission read:

“Found on wasteland near derelict station at place of incident at 18:30 hours. Brought in by ambulance. Violent assault from unknown assailant. Tibia and fibula left leg shattered. Pinned.”

Dave wasn’t very good at anatomy, but from the description, he presumed that he had done an excellent job of smashing Blackwell’s leg to smithereens. There was a long spell in ITU where he had caught sepsis after his operation. Now he was going to the ward. The plan was rehabilitation for a week and then home. But Dave was very interested in the front page of his notes; there was no one listed as his next of kin! Dave flicked through the notes to the first entry, from 1986. He had ended up in hospital with a fractured tibia and fibula from an injury sustained at work. Apparently an axe had fallen on his leg! Dave grinned to himself…there it was, the name at the top of the page was “Leslie Blackwell” not “Leslie Greenwell!” He had made up a cock and bull story, and definitely hadn’t reported Dave – as he suspected, Blackwell and Evans had covered the whole thing up!

Dave emerged from the cubicle cautiously. Satisfied that he was alone in the toilet he hid the notes behind his apron. He left the toilet and walked back over to where Blackwell was. He bent down and slipped the notes back under the wheelchair. As he did so, something fell out of the bag containing Blackwell’s personal belongings - a door key. Dave picked it up and placed it in his pocket.

This time, he, Dave Williams, was in control! And a plan was beginning to form in his head. He pushed Blackwell back to the ward, resisting the urge to let him fall down the steps leading to the downstairs level just outside, and then headed back up to the porters’ office.

‘Ajay, it’s time for a cup of tea.’

‘I agree, Dave, it’s been hours.’

Dave felt invincible. Now he not only had absolute confirmation of Blackwell's address, but he also had a way in. All day, he spent his spare moments dreaming of methods that he could use to cause Leslie Blackwell more serious harm. A myriad of possibilities ran through his mind over the last few hours of his shift. These ranged from using sharp weapons to poisoning Blackwell's dinner on the ward.

Dave thought back to the first time – when he had smashed the axe into Blackwell's shin. The look on Blackwell's face, and that evil bastard, Evans. He had taken a massive gamble. He fully expected to be in deep trouble and be arrested, but he hadn't been, had he? Then when he had done it again, nobody was looking for him! If he had got away with it twice, maybe could get away with it again? Plus that had been easy. Back then, the first time, it had been a Hobson's choice – he had had no choice. The second time he couldn't help himself. But now? Things were different, he had a lot to lose. What would he do if he was taken from Audrey? His girls? And put in a cell with lots of time to think? Surely he would crack up? Plus, he felt that he'd moved on. If he did something to Blackwell and got caught, he would indirectly ruin his own life for good. Dave couldn't bear to think about it. Would he get sent to jail for a long time? Lose his job? What if it all went wrong and he hurt someone else?

Dave either had to forget all about it, or devise a plan, a plan so watertight that he would be untraceable.

'Jeez, it sounds like the folk sending these emails know about as much about it all as I do. All I can fathom is if you stay away from it, you're OK!' said Ajay as he read yet another alert about coronavirus.

'But if you don't, you're sometimes not.'

For the last couple of months, Dave had avoided the topic of coronavirus. It made him feel both depressed and demoralised. Suddenly, he began to feel interested in it: *What exactly was it? How did it work? How did you catch it? How long did it live on ordinary surfaces?* He began to read the emails that he hadn't read properly from the last few weeks. Work had not yet started to pick up tonight so he had a bit of time. He searched on his phone; it was an RNA virus. What did that mean? It meant that it got into your body, and stole cells to replicate. What no one knew for sure is what exactly it did, but it seemed to attack the tissues of the lungs and airway. People had strange symptoms like loss of taste and smell. It was supposed to get worse from days seven–ten, but they had patients that had been on ventilators for a couple of weeks and the swabs kept coming up positive, maybe because now they felt that it was to do with the amount of viral load – so if you kept breathing the same load in and out in the same dirty air (like on a plane, or in an air conditioned building, or the same dirty room where the same air was being recycled) you would get sicker and sicker.

Dave read through the new emails. Most of it was about protective equipment, cross contamination, no-go areas, safe transportation of patients and other stuff.

Linen from the COVID ward had to be moved in full PPE. Clinical waste was transported safely and linen was sent for a boil wash. Dave began to think hard about things. What if the dirty linen got in to someone's house? Someone who should be staying in and self-isolating with a bad chest? Someone who lived on their own so that no one else could be affected? But then what if someone else did go to that person's house? Or an infected person went to a public area where there were innocent people around? Or got sick and was brought into hospital? That could be a disaster. No, that plan was crazy, he needed another one – a better one.

Dave pulled his phone out and googled "Leslie Blackwell paedophile". There they were, the allegations dating from the 1990s. He had served time in prison for child abuse. There were convictions from other areas; Manchester, London, York. He had clearly travelled around, surely he hadn't operated alone? Just with Evans? There was more, he had been sent back to prison in 2007 for repeated offences. And again in 2013. He was obviously a prolific offender. Dave wondered how long he had been out for this time. Dave googled "Leslie Greenwell paedophile". Nothing came up. Since he had changed his name, he had obviously been lying low.

That evening on his way home from work, Dave took a diversion to Ken's new flat. Ken had not yet moved in and Elle had bought him some lightbulbs and other hardware to put up. Dave put a mask on and went inside to sort them out. The garden below backed onto the beginning of the complex where Leslie Blackwell lived. The fence outside was an old wooden one. A few of the panels had fallen down and there was a gap in the hedge where someone had made an unofficial pathway through. When the estate was new, the sheltered accommodation was for older people only. Now they were for people who were classed as being “vulnerable”. Not just with physical disabilities, but people with all manner of problems. This ranged from drug addicts to people with severe mental health problems like Ken. Often the pairing of such people in the same area was highly inappropriate. He shuddered at the thought of Leslie Blackwell being placed next to vulnerable people. What would he do to them? Would he abuse them just like he had abused the children that he was supposed to be looking after in the home? Steal from them? As Dave looked out over the garden below, ideas began to form in his head. He sincerely hoped that Ken never realised who was living in the bungalow behind him. Thank goodness there was a lockdown!

Friday 1st May 2020

Ken was now home and had settled in his flat. Dave hoped that he would stay for longer in this one than he had stayed in his previous accommodation. He was shielding. His medication was being delivered from the pharmacy and Dave and Elle were doing his shopping. As per the rules, Dave was not allowed to go into the flat, he had to stay outside to speak to Ken, or join him for a quick chat in the garden below.

Dave was super-careful when it came to Ken. He would drop off his shopping and have a chat to him in the garden. It was difficult to ask Ken how he was and expect an honest reply, as there was no privacy. Dave worried that Ken wasn't telling him how his mental health was for fear of the whole building overhearing. Working in the hospital, transporting patients with known diagnoses of COVID-19 from ward to ward, to the mortuary, encountering dirty linen and so on, made Dave paranoid about putting Ken at risk of contracting anything from him. He even took his own cup round to Ken's, and, wearing a glove, poured the tea that Ken had made him into it, handing the empty cup back to Ken. With his liver in a mess and his immunity low, Ken was at high risk of contracting COVID-19 and had been advised by his doctor to shield for the foreseeable future.

Dave felt sorry for everyone who lived in the flats. There were older people who were shielding or following very strict social distancing guidelines. Then there were people like Ken who seemed to be just normal people – at first. But when Ken had got to know them, he had found that they too had severe mental health problems, or other issues. Every couple of days Dave went shopping for Ken, left his groceries outside in a disinfected carrier bag and told him to wipe everything down once it was inside the house.

When Ken came into the garden to see him they sat two metres apart. They weren't really supposed to meet in the garden, but if Ken had no contact with him, Dave worried about him relapsing. Ken was still on methadone and while he had been in hospital and rehabilitation he had stopped injecting drugs and drinking alcohol. But with drug dealers around the estate losing business from people not going to pubs and clubs, and county lines systems finding it hard to operate, they were desperately looking for easy prey to peddle their wares to. Ken was easy prey.

From the garden, Dave could see through the back of the hedge into the complex where Blackwell lived. Over the last few weeks, Dave had studied the area meticulously. Rather than going around the front as the whole street was monitored with CCTV cameras, Dave realised that he could easily sneak through the hedges at the back of Ken's flat and cross into the garden unseen.

He spent his spare time fantasising about the possibilities. Should he spike Blackwell's food with poison? No, that would be too quick and not painful enough. Electrocute him? So that by the time anyone found him he would be burned to a crisp? Na, too quick. He could always set fire to his bungalow, lock him in and watch him burn through the window? That would be brilliant, but too risky! Blackwell was probably shielding, and therefore wouldn't be going far; it wasn't even as if Dave could wait for him anywhere. And he was no longer very mobile. Whatever it was going to be it was going to be slow, protracted, painful, torturous.

'So, how've you been?' he asked Ken as they sat in the back garden two metres apart.

'OK, at first, it was nice to be locked away from the world. But I'm feeling a bit, well, down with it all now. I've started hearing the voices again.'

Dave's heart sank. The fact that Ken was disclosing this to him as they sat in the garden within earshot of the whole complex meant that he must be bad. When he heard voices, it usually meant that he was sinking into a psychotic depression where eventually the voices would start telling him that he was better off dead. The only way that he could stop them and make himself feel any better was by self-medicating with alcohol and heroin.

When Ken told him about the voices, they sounded like people from the past. Bad people. People who Ken had possibly encountered in the home. How Dave wished that he and Ken had not been split up, so that he could understand what Ken meant by them. Dave didn't dare ask Ken directly about who they were, or what they had done, so as not to cause him any unnecessary distress. Ken had declined to go back to mental health services. When he had first disclosed his abuse after leaving care he hadn't been believed. Afterwards, he had received counselling where he was encouraged to keep talking about the past. He said that it was just awful: all it had done was drag it all up again and again and again. Dave could understand this, this was how he felt about it all. He didn't want to discuss his previous experience with anyone.

'Can I ask you just one question, Ken, are the voices people from the home?'

Ken nodded slowly, but he didn't elaborate. Dave knew not to probe.

Dave had always known why he did what he did; his heart sank. Nothing would ever make Ken better. If Blackwell and Evans had done what they had done to the other kids there, he needed to forget about it. And when the voices were forcing their way into his consciousness, drinking and taking drugs were the only things that made him forget. Then he became ill and needed to dry out. Then when he was sober and in a straight frame of mind, the slightest thing that made him remember it tipped him off again. It was the same cycle that Ken had been in his whole life and Dave could see it starting again, sooner rather than later. Nothing had ever stopped it before, not even his beautiful daughter, or his wife who had tried her best to help him. Dave knew that Ken was experiencing hell on earth. Sometimes, when he was completely tortured, the drink and drugs no longer worked, and when he had exhausted every other maladaptive coping method possible, he would try to commit suicide. Luckily, someone had always found him. Should Ken ever succeed, he would finally be at peace. Dave hated himself for acknowledging that.

'Got a lot to answer for, our mum and the tosspot that was our dad, haven't they?' Ken said.

Dave nodded. 'I just don't get it. How can you treat your kids like that? And actually kill someone? When I saw our two, I knew from the moment our Lisa was born, that if anyone ever touched a hair of her head I'd murder them, they'd be a gonner.'

Ken didn't reply.

'And the thought of leavin' them, alone, Christ, I'd rather die with them myself. I can't imagine myself leavin' them in the freezing cold, in their underwear, holdin' onto a threadbare duvet, while I buy myself bottles of wine, then sell myself on the streets to buy more.'

Ken shook his head. 'I never think of her as my mum, I always remember Nan as being my mum.'

'Me too. I doubt either of us would be here if it wasn't for Nan, would we?'

'I wish they'd never had me, Dave. I'm just glad Karen had her head screwed on when we had Elle. I've been no better than them, have I?'

'Ken, I didn't mean it like that...'

'No. I put myself first, the drugs, she'd have been no better than we were if it had been left up to me. It took me a long time to admit that to myself. Look at you. You had a bad time, you ended up in that home too! It was that bad you ran away. You were a real dad to your kids, not like me.'

'Mate, I was only there less than a week. That was enough for me. If I'd have had to stay there, I'd be doing exactly what you do to forget.'

'You've been a real dad to your kids, not like me. I should have stepped up but I didn't. I wish I could be that happy, but I could never settle, I was always looking for an easy fix, something to numb the pain.'

Dave didn't speak. He had already said too much. He didn't usually talk about their mum and dad, or the past. It would undoubtedly drive them both mad if they let it. So Dave usually tried to talk about the present, the future, anything except the past.

'Anyway, when the flaming heck do you think Man City will be able to play again?' he asked.

Ken shrugged. 'God knows!'

Dave shuddered. He looked over at the top of Blackwell's bungalow and prayed that Ken would never find out that he lived there.

Saturday May 2nd 2020

It was Dave's day off. Free Saturdays usually involved shopping or walking with Audrey and a trip down to the local social club for a pint while they watched the football. But lockdown ensured that usual rituals had been abandoned. Dave had been surprised about his indifference to the situation and how he had managed to fill his time up with other, more important activities. Later he planned to take Stacy for a walk up the hills towards the mountain. She loved going up there.

Emma was working today. She was still in college until she had been sent home in March. Now with lessons online she had taken on more hours in her job in the local corner shop.

The sunken garden lawn was appearing slowly but surely. The sides had been built up with rubble and topped with soil left over from the garden. Dave's plan was to continue building up the sides so that Audrey could plant flowers and bushes. Stacy busied herself with her bucket and spade, playing in the mud. The garden felt peaceful, and private and regenerated. With the sunken garden and a six-foot fence running around the perimeter, nobody could see them except for next door.

Dave planned to make some pergolas out of the excess wood that he had lying around. If he could get them up and get some climbers growing round them, it would take off in the next year or so.

Nowhere had any plants for sale, so Dave decided that he would just have to make use of what they had left in the garden. Barry and Sheila next door were avid gardeners and had some lovely plants. They had already given quite a few to Dave.

'Barry, is there any chance that I can have a cutting off your rhododendron, mate?'

'Well, funny enough, Ron over the way was asking me the other day if I had anything to swap,' said Barry. 'No one can get anything for the garden anywhere! And it's the only bloody place any of us can go! Everyone wants their garden looking nice, don't they? Let's face it, none of us have got anything better to do. If you've got any topsoil spare, I'd like a bit.'

'No problem, mate, I'll bring you some round. I know, sad aren't we?' said Dave. 'But I'm all up for swapping stuff if anyone's got anything spare. I'm gonna grow some sunflowers with the little one,'

'Aww, she'll love that! She'll love having her own flowers'.

'I know, they're cute at this age, ain't they?'

After lugging a wheelbarrow of topsoil over to Barry's, Dave sprinkled some more of his grass seed over the garden and watered it. Then he and Stacy planted the sunflowers.

His next job was to build her a little den to play in. When the girls were younger, Dave had made them all kinds of stuff. They'd had endless hours of fun playing in his creations.

Audrey had been dying to get rid of an old cupboard in the house for god knew how long. Dave carried it out into the garden. He made some stilts for it, put it on the top of them and covered it over with some old wood and tin sheeting that he had from inside the shed. Brilliant, now Stacy had her own little den.

That evening it was warm, and sunny - just like being abroad. It was barbeque night. Baz and Sheila pulled up their chairs by the wall and they all had a drink in the garden. Audrey had been baking cakes with Stacy so they had pudding after. Nobody cared that they weren't in a caravan in Rhyl, or in a hotel in Spain, or on a yacht in Tenerife, this was all they needed. Everyone was chilled, everyone was happy. But, try as he might, whenever Dave thought about Ken, he just couldn't shake the feeling that something bad was about to happen.

Thursday 14th May 2020

On his way home from work, Dave made a detour to Ken's to drop off some cigarettes. He knocked on the door, but Ken didn't answer. Then he noticed the milk that he had left for Ken yesterday was still there. Dave knocked again – nothing. He phoned Ken, but there was no reply. Dave phoned Elle; she didn't reply either. He began to panic.

'Ken! Ken!' he yelled through the letter box. No reply.

Dave didn't have a key, the only person who did was Elle. His fingers shaking, he dialled her number again – still no answer. He had a really bad feeling about this; he had been worrying about Ken for a couple of days, never quite shaking off the feeling that something wasn't quite right. In desperation, Dave rang the police and waited until they came.

'Thanks for coming, it's my brother. He's not well; I take him food, but he hasn't taken in the milk I left him last night, now he's not answering the door.'

The police officers looked at each other.

'Is there anybody else you can phone?'

'Well, only his daughter, my niece, but I can't get hold of her. Look, he's an alcoholic, he's got severely bad mental health, and he's in end stage liver failure, do you know what I mean?'

Eventually, the police put on their protective clothing, broke the door down and went into the flat with Dave staying outside. As soon as they opened the door, he could see Ken lying on the floor, surrounded by bottles of vodka and drug paraphernalia.

'Oh my god! Is he dead?'

'No, he's still breathing.'

'Ken? Ken? Can you hear me?' said Dave. 'Ken… wake up…'

The police called an ambulance and wrapped Ken up in a blanket. He was barely conscious. His eyes were intermittently rolling up into the back of his head.

'Ken! What the bloody hell's wrong?'

Ken was no longer able to walk. His legs were swollen. The policemen went outside to speak to the ambulance crew. Inside, Ken lay on the floor looking yellower than ever. Dave knelt next to him.

'It's no good, Dave, I went back on it. I couldn't stay off it. I just can't do it!'

'Mate, why didn't you say something?'

Ken shook his head. 'They've got me, Dave. They've ended up killing me.'

'Who? Who has, Ken?'

'The ones from the home. I see their faces every time I shut my eyes.'

Dave desperately wanted to put his arms around Ken, and cuddle him, and tell him that everything was going to be OK. But he couldn't.

'Ken, it's bloody dangerous in the hospital mate, there's rona everywhere, pal! That's the last place you should be going! I shouldn't be standing here, so close!'

Ken nodded his head.

'I know, Dave, but I can't stay at home, I'm too far gone. I can't live here, normally. I'm not normal, I never will be.' Tears began to drip down his face.

'Ken, if you go in, you might not come back out!'

'I hope it does get me, I can't stand this lockdown stuff. I can't bear just stayin' in that flat on my own, thinking about it all, over and over again.'

'It's not like before, I can't come and see you, visit you! They're not allowing visitors, on the ward!'

Ken nodded. 'I know, mate, I can't see me comin' out this time. I've written a letter to say goodbye to Elle, last night I even phoned Karen and apologised to her for being such an arse to her all these years, her and Elle! She must have thought it was just cos I was off me face. But they've got me, mate. I just can't forget!'

'Please, don't leave me! I love you, mate! You're my big brother!'

'Thanks for everything you've done for me. I love you, man! It... it should have been me looking after you.' Ken began to sob.

'It doesn't matter does it, mate?' said Dave, holding Ken in his arms.

'But it's time for me to go. I've written it all down for you anyway. I sent it to yours.'

Dave began to sob. Last time that Ken had written him a letter, he had tried to hang himself from a beam in a garage. But the chair that he had gone to stand on had been rotten and he had ended up breaking his ankle instead. Ken had planned this. He clearly had no intention of coming back to his flat, he was perfectly serious this time. If he had written a letter, he must have had some kind of an inkling that he was either so unwell that he was going to die, or he fully intended to kill himself.

Dave knew that Ken didn't have long left regardless of his relapse. He was no doctor, but anyone who was that yellow, and full of fluid, and low with it all, surely must have organs shutting down? He already had hepatitis and liver failure from all the drug use. And the worst part of it was, none of it was his fault. In the end, the system which was supposed to protect him had failed him. Violated him. Ruined him like it had done to others, like it could have so easily done to Dave. And there was nothing that Dave or anyone else could do to help him, Ken was way beyond help. Ken looked up at Dave, his eyeballs yellow, his eyes soulless.

'I'm going, Dave, I'm ready. But know how much I love you. I'm sorry I couldn't look after you when you needed me.'

'Ken, it wasn't your fault! It was Mum and Dad's. They're the ones that should have looked after us. I never meant it, all them years ago when I said it. I love you, just know that.'

'I love you too, Dave! Come here. I'm dying, Dave, please, just let me hold you again.'

The two paramedics came in wearing their protective clothing. They looked at Ken and Dave just like the paramedics who had come to take their nan to the hospital all those years ago had looked at them, their eyes filled with sympathy and pity. Dave waited for them to shout at them for touching each other, for risking spreading the disease. What the hell did it matter now? They were all thinking the same thing. Time rewound. Dave was a kid again. He could see his his nan. The flashbacks, the memories, the intrusive thoughts returned. Try as he might, he couldn't let Ken go, not like he had just let his nan go in the ambulance.

'Look, we're going to put him in the ambulance in a minute. Do you want to have two minutes before we do so?' Dave nodded. They left Ken just inside the doorway and went down to the ambulance.

'Just hold me, Dave, just for one last time.'

They were six and seven and a half years old again and the police and ambulance crew were at their old house on the estate in Manchester where they were snuggled under the grotty duvet cover trying to keep warm. Years melted away, and Dave felt safe with Ken. Just for a few minutes.

'She was ace, Nan, wasn't she? I'm jealous that you're goin' to see her, you know. When you get to the other side, tell her I love her? Not that she needs telling, she knew anyway.'

'She was. She'd have been so proud of you, the way you've brought the girls up, and looked out for me and Elle. She did a good job on you, Dave. Me? I think I had too much of Mum and Dad in me.'

'Na, you just had the misfortune of seeing things you shouldn't have, plus, you never got to say goodbye to Nan like I did. Like I say though, I'm jealous you're going to get to see her. I love you so much.'

Elle arrived at the door.

'Dad.'

'Quick, Elle, say your goodbyes, he's really ill. They're coming back to take him in a minute. I love you, Ken.'

On the way out, Dave spoke to the paramedics. 'This is my brother, Ken, please take good care of him. We had the worst beginning imaginable, that's why he, you know, takes the drugs, why he's like this.'

'Don't worry, we'll look after him.'

They waited a few moments more as Elle said her final goodbyes to her dad. Then they took him down the stairs and into the ambulance. Dave and Elle stood and watched, feeling helpless. The door shut and Ken was gone. Dave felt relieved that Elle had managed to see him before he had been taken, but he had a bad feeling that it was the last time that he would ever see his brother.

Dave walked home in a daze. That night, he tossed and turned, trying to switch everything off. He was angry, about the unfairness, about the fact that Ken had had no chance in life. Thoughts of him and Ken whirled around and around in his head; when he shut his eyes, he saw his mum and dad, his nan, Blackwell, Evans.

The next day, the post came. There was a letter addressed to Dave.

To my dear brother, well, I wasn't much of a big brother to you, was I? I should have been there to look out for you and stop you going in that home.

They've got me, Ken, I just want to go and be with Nan. I can't be normal.

There were others, but these were the ringleaders;

Leslie Blackwell, Raymond Evans.

Please, make sure they never go near Elle or any of the others. If you ever find them, make sure you do them over for me.

Sorry for all the hurt and trouble I've caused over the years. I'll give Nan a kiss for you.

I love you so much,

Your brother Ken.

Dave held the letter firmly as tears dripped down his face. He knew that it was probably the last thing that Ken would ever give him, except worry and heartache. Blackwell and Evans! How had those same two devils who had tried to torture him been allowed to get to Ken too? How had they wrecked so many children's lives? Robbing them of any normality and leaving them with scars that never healed?

Maybe he could go to the police? But that would take many years. Plus, they had already been prosecuted. It was too late now for Ken to tell his story – now he'd never have his say! His closure! Maybe Dave could try and find Evans too? Put a balaclava on and go round with a baseball bat?

All day, Dave stayed outside in the garden, chain smoking and drinking endless cups of coffee. Ruminating. Everybody presumed that he was worried about Ken. He was worried, but he was also raging. He thought he'd had his revenge, put it all back to bed, ruined Blackwell's life like Blackwell had ruined his. But what about Ken? Where was his justice? They'd near enough killed him.

Dave did not sleep well again. He barely grabbed more than a couple of hours sleep before his alarm went off and it was time to go back to work. When he got to work, he called Ken's ward.

'How is he?"

'He's not too bad, just comfortable at the moment. He's really not well though, Dave.'

'I know I can't see him, can I Facetime him?'

'Well, we'll give it a go later, but to be honest, I don't know if he's capable.'

Dave walked up to the ward and dropped some things off for Ken with Ann, one of the healthcare assistants.

'How is he, Ann? I can't come and see him, do you think he's bad?'

Ann nodded. 'He's quite out of it at the moment, Dave. A bit unresponsive. Do you want me to try and see if I can Facetime you?'

'Please, Ann, even if it's just to say goodbye.'

'Dave, I'd love to let you in, but I can't.'

'I know you can't, Ann.'

'Aww, I'd give you a hug if I could Dave, but I can't!'

'I know. Look, Ann, Ken's been shielding for the last few weeks. I've bin fetching him stuff. I know I'm a risk, but he's dying, isn't he?'

Ann looked up at Dave, her eyes filled with sympathy over her mask.

'Just wait here, Dave, give me a few minutes. Just bring a wheelchair.'

Dave waited outside the ward and tried to compose himself as Ann reappeared.

'Dave, we need a patient transported to ward 6Y. Are you able to do it?' She winked.

He nodded.

'Get some PPE on and come with me.'

Dave washed his hands, put his personal protective equipment on and followed Ann through the ward. She arrived at a bed and pulled the curtains round.

'This is Mr. Oakes, he just happens to need to go to ward 7Y.' Then her voice changed to a whisper. 'He also just happens to be in the next bed to your Ken, so if you accidentally pulled the curtains back - you'd probably see him. I'll be back in five minutes with his notes.' She winked over the top of her mask.

Dave's heart leapt. 'Ann, you're a bloody legend!'

Dave opened the curtains to see Ken. There he was, bloated, his skin mottled, sedated due to the pain. He was dying.

'Ken, it's me, Dave.' Ken wrapped his fingers around Dave's hand.

'How are you?'

'OK,' he whispered. 'I'm dyin', Dave.'

A large lump formed in Dave's throat.

'I know. I got your letter, the one about Blackwell and Evans. I know who they are, Ken. One's got a limp. You ever seen him on a stick?'

Ken nodded slowly.

'That was me, I broke his leg with an iron bar. He's back in here. I smashed his other leg up in the park the other week,' he whispered.

Ken smiled and squeezed his hand tighter.

'Don't you worry, Ken, you'll have your justice. Even if you're not here to see it, I'll know you'll be up there, watching from above. I love you, mate.' Dave bent down to kiss Ken. Ken opened his eyes slightly and looked up at him.

'I love you, brother,' he whispered as he shut his eyes again.

Dave hugged Ken tightly. 'Do something for me, Dave…'

'Anything.'

'Make sure that they scatter me over the beach where Nan used to take us in the caravan? Remember… when we lived with her? When we used to go to all them arcades… and have fun on the beach… and the big water-centre there? The one with the slide an' the monorail?'

'I know, I loved it there, mate. We used to take the girls there in a caravan; remember I took Elle a couple of times, do you remember? They used to love it!'

Ken smiled and clutched Dave's hand tighter.

'I remember her telling me… leathered as I was… I felt happy that at least one of us could… you know, take her there.'

Ken's voice was now a mere whisper as he fought for breath. Dave held him tightly, kissing him on the head. Ann didn't usually work down here on this ward, but she must have been working an extra shift; he doubted that anybody else would have accidentally on purpose arranged for him to see his brother. This was the last time that he would ever see him. He was damned if he wasn't going to hold him for one last time, to tell him how much he loved him, to comfort him. Eventually, after much longer than five minutes, Ann reappeared.

'Sorry, Dave, I left it as long as I could. Sister's on the warpath.'

'Goodbye, Ken, I love you brother.' Dave gave Ken's hand one last squeeze and cradled his head in his arms.

'I love you, Dave.'

'Give Nan a squeeze from me, bud. Sleep tight.'

Dave pulled the curtains around Ken for the last time.

'Chuck your PPE in here, Dave,' said Ann, indicating a bin. 'Are you OK?'

Dave nodded. 'Yeah, I'm fine, just a bit choked up, but thanks, Ann, I'll never forget that, that I had the chance to say goodbye. He's gonna die soon. I can't tell you how much it means to me. Look, I'm going to go and have a quick shower and change into my spare uniform before I come back and get Mr. Oakes, OK?'

'Dave, I'd hug you if I could, you look like you need one, but I can't.'

'I know, love, I know.'

'Just be quick, or Sister will wonder where you've gone.'

'Give me five minutes, love, and I'll be back.'

'I'll make up an excuse'

Just as he was about to finish his shift, Dave got a call from the ward to say that Ken had passed away. Later, when Dave saw Ann, she told him that when it had come to the end, she had sat with him and held his hand for the last few moments. She had spoken to him about Dave before he had slipped into unconsciousness. The last thing that he told her was to tell Dave he was going to see Nan and he would give her a hug from him. Dave took great comfort in knowing that Ken hadn't died alone.

As he walked home, overcome with grief, tears poured down his cheeks. He felt that people must have thought that he was a right weirdo, walking along the road, crying. He no longer cared. A strange emotion swept over him. Dave felt sad, so sad. It was a strange feeling, a weird feeling of being left on the planet all alone with nobody left from where you came from, nobody who remembered you as a child. Like an odd, extinct creature. But it was a strange dichotomy of sadness and severance. Severance with the past, with everything bad that had ever happened to him. Dave had created new life, a new family, all of his own. A family that he had loved, and nurtured, together with Elle who he had treated like his own. Dave felt so grateful that he had his girls. But he also felt guilty. Guilty because part of him felt relieved now that Ken was at peace.

But why was he, Dave still here? What was so special about him? Why had he not had the bad time that Ken had had? What right did he have to not see his mum lying dead on the floor like Ken did? And have to spend less time in the godforsaken home? Maybe it was his fault that Ken had died. Maybe he should have helped him more. If he had, maybe Ken would still be here now. *Stop it, Dave, you'll go insane*. Stemming from the injustice, the guilt, slowly but surely, anger and agitation grew in Dave.

As the hours and days passed, the anger grew to volcanic proportions. And even more determined because he had made a promise to Ken, Dave formed his plan.

Saturday May 16th 2020

Dave could see on the patient list on the main computer that Blackwell had been moved to another ward. He knew exactly where he'd gone. Dave hadn't been called to that specific ward, but he was on his way. When he entered, Blackwell had positioned himself in the middle of the entrance in his wheelchair, looking miserable and glum.

When he spotted Dave, Blackwell said, 'I'm bored, can't you get me out of here? Or at least wheel me round the hospital or somat?'

'No. Anyway, what you doing in a public area? Don't you know you're supposed to be in by your bed?'

Andi, the nurse on the station, rolled her eyes as she returned to the desk, noting that Blackwell had once again moved out of his bay.

'Leslie! Get back in to your bed, for the last time. One more time and I'm getting security to remove you! From this hospital!'

Blackwell swore under his breath, his face was like thunder. He reluctantly wheeled himself back into the bay where his bed was. Dave used all the power that he had within him to stop himself from grabbing the man out of his chair and hitting him so hard that he would fly straight across the ward.

'Some people have got no idea have they, Dave?' she said. 'I'm sorry to hear about your brother; Ann told me last time she was down here.'

'Ahh, thanks. I thought about not coming in, but it just makes it worse, you know, sitting there, thinking about it all, about the horrible time we had when we were kids, about Ken…'

Andi listened sympathetically to Dave.

'Sorry to go on… Anyway, I'd have thought he would have gone home by now.' Dave gestured over to Blackwell as he sat in his wheelchair, staring evilly at them both for asking him to move.

'Na, he doesn't want to go really, why would he? He's got everything getting done for him here – washing him, his dinner, a nice warm place. God, he's horrible. He nearly got chucked out yesterday for saying disgusting things to one of the healthcare assistants while she was washing him.'

'Jeez, dirty sod. Have you got any background on him? Do you know if he usually does stuff like that? He could be the biggest perv going.'

Andi shook her head.

'Na, we don't really know much about him at all. All we know is that he's horrible, he lives on his own, and he doesn't seem to have any family. No one ever phones about him, apart from some bloke called Reg now and again, and there's no next of kin listed.

'Oi, nurse.' Shouted Blackwell, indignantly from across the ward.

Andi ignored him. 'God, we can't wait for him to go. All he does is moan at us all day long; he's just rude and takes time from patients who really need us.'

A bloke called Reg! How interesting! Dave thought. Dave had to think on his feet here. He didn't want anyone to know that he knew Leslie Blackwell. If anyone suspected, all of his carefully laid plans would be thwarted.

'Yeah, he does look dodgy, doesn't he? Like the type who's got a past. What's his name? Leslie Blackwell?'

She shook her head. 'No, Leslie Greenwell.'

'Funny that, I'm sure someone told me his name was Leslie Blackwell...'

'We did check up with social services to look at health and support needs when he goes home; they haven't got any record of him though. One of the other patients recognised him, said he thought he looked like someone who worked in a care home and used to abuse kids. He said he was called the wrong name though.'

'One of the other staff members was telling me about him, can't remember who it was now, Leslie Blackwell, that's definitely what they said his name is. Funny enough, they said something to me something about him working in a dodgy care home.' Lied Dave.

‘Really? Leslie Blackwell? That’s strange, we’ve got his name down as Leslie Greenwell…’

‘Hmmm, that’s weird, they definitely said it was Leslie Blackwell. I bet he’s changed his name if he’s dodgy, though. I bet he doesn’t want anyone to know who he is. I’m rubbish with technology, but I bet if you search “Leslie Blackwell” and “care home”, you’ll find something dodgy… he looks just the type.’

Dave could see the look on the Andi’s face. He had managed to plant a seed. A seed of doubt. She wanted to know more.

‘Well, I’ll have a look in a minute,’ she said as she pulled her phone out.

A small smile crept across Dave’s face. That was one thing he had remembered not seeing in the notes. And now Andi had confirmed to him that he had no next of kin. Well, well, well! That meant Blackwell had no one looking out for him should anything happen. How terribly sad. But then Blackwell would know all about that; looking out for vulnerable people with no next of kin was one of his specialities when he worked in the children’s home.

‘Anyway, which ward did you need me to go to and who do you want me to take?’

‘Aw?’ said Andi looking up at him in surprise. ‘Nobody, Dave.’

‘Aww,’ said Dave looking surprised and checking his bleep. ‘Aww, sorry, Andi, I’ve come to the wrong ward. Sorry, not thinking straight, got, you know, a lot going on and all that.’

Andi looked at him sympathetically. ‘I know, Dave.’

‘Anyway, if he’s causing you a load of problems on the ward, or you need him shifting quickly, just bleep, ask for me, and I’ll come as soon as I can, get him out your hair like.’

‘Thanks, Dave. The sooner he goes the better!’

‘Anytime.’ He walked off, grinning to himself behind his mask like a Cheshire cat – his plan was working so far.

Sunday May 17th 2020

The next day the bleep went off in the porter's office, and Andi asked specifically for Dave.

'Him there, to x-ray please, Dave, it's a follow up x-ray to make sure that his pin is in place, he keeps complaining about the pain. I'm sure he is in pain, don't get me wrong, but he moans that much about everything, it's hard to know with him whether he's genuine or not!'

On hearing how much pain Blackwell was in, an inappropriately large smile crept across Dave's face under his mask.

'And when you come back, come and find me. I've got something very interesting to tell you...'

Dave could barely contain himself – he was dying to know what it was that Andi had found out. The large smile turned to a full blown grin as Dave wheeled Blackwell off happily to x-ray, whistling as he went.

'So, home soon is it, mate?'

'Yeah,' replied Blackwell grumpily.

'Well, that's good then, innit?'

'No. They say I'll never walk properly again. I'd love to get that guy who jumped me. Flamin' police weren't interested.'

Underneath his mask, Dave's grin spread further across his face. He had never, ever been so glad to have a mask on. Under normal circumstances Leslie Blackwell would have seen him by now and realised who he was. But by the grace of COVID-19, here Dave was, in a mask, gleaning information from one of the two people that he hated the most in the world.

'Aw, aye. Yeah, establishments, eh? Rotten to the core, ain't they? Can't trust any of them, can you?'

Leslie Blackwell shook his head.

'So have you got someone to look after you? You know, when you get home and all that?'

He shook his head again.

'No. Got a mate, Reg, who brings me stuff round now and again. I'm on my own. I don't want to go home. What if they come back? What if they know where I live?'

Dave revelled in the fact that Leslie Blackwell was running scared. His heart began to beat faster at the mention of the name "Reg".

'He sounds like a good mate, does he live far from you?'

Blackwell shook his head. 'Yeah, known him for years, we used to work together. Na, just a few streets away.'

Palpitations and fear rose up in Dave's chest as he remembered the amount of power that Reginald Evans had once held over him, and how close he came to violating him like Leslie Blackwell had tried to. And he lived by Blackwell? Just down the road! Dave began to shudder at the thought, then he tried to rationalise it all in his mind. But Reginald Evans must be knocking on, mid-seventies, or eighty by now? What was there to be scared of? If he was anywhere near as debilitated and decrepit as Leslie Blackwell, he would be absolutely no threat whatsoever.

Well, what an interesting morning he had had!

Blackwell was silent for the rest of the journey. Dave left him in the x-ray department and asked the staff to bleep him specifically when they needed him to be picked up again. He was interested to know what Andi had found out. A short while later he was bleeped back.

'Jeez,' said the lady behind the desk in x-ray, 'he's a bundle of joy isn't he? All he's done is moan and swear since he got out of there because he's had to wait a couple of minutes for his x-ray! Then he was moaning about having to wait for you. He's shut up now though, thank goodness.'

Dave rolled his eyeballs.

'Aw, he's not a very nice man, not a very nice man at all, take it from me.'

Blackwell was sitting quietly. As he looked, Dave noticed a little boy waiting for an x-ray with his mum on the chair opposite. Blackwell was watching him, fixated, leering. It was obvious, surely even the little boy's mum had noticed.

'Is it just me, or is he staring at that kid?' said Dave to the lady behind the desk.

She put her head up over the counter and looked.

'Definitely. No, he definitely is!'

'Thought so.'

Dave strode over to Blackwell.

'Right, we're ready to go back,' he said as he began to take the brakes off the chair.

'Well, there's no rush,' said Blackwell as he continued to fixate on the little boy.

The mum of the little boy looked up at Dave, fear on her face.

'Do you know this little boy, Leslie?'

'What? Er, no.'

'He... he's... been staring at him, and saying...things, not very nice things. I'm glad he's going, he's made me feel very uncomfortable,' said the boy's mum.

'I, er, well, I'm just being friendly.'

'Well you need to stop doing it, Leslie, you're obviously making this lady uncomfortable.'

'You're disgusting! I've a good mind to report you to the police! Who can I complain to?'

'Lady behind the desk, love.' Dave winked at the woman.

She marched over to the x-ray department clerk taking her little boy with her.

Feeling sick to the pit of his stomach at the prospect of Leslie Blackwell still having access to children, Dave started to wheel him back to the ward quickly.

'God, I'm sick of this flaming place! Bloody bitch in there, I was only bein' friendly!'

Dave didn't reply. He would ensure that the lady behind the reception desk made a formal complaint that was recorded. Maybe the little boy's mum would even report him to the police if what he had said was that bad. Dave tried not to engage in any further conversation with Blackwell for the duration of the journey through the hospital corridors. But Blackwell clearly wanted to vent.

'They've said I can only get about in a wheelchair long distance from now on… I'd love to find whoever it was that did my leg in!'

Dave smirked to himself. Oh dear. Blackwell would have to cancel his visits to the working girls and boys in the park for the foreseeable future. There would be no kids playing in the park outside anymore that he would find it easy to engage with, and he wouldn't even be able to get to the supermarket. If Dave could have, he would have patted himself on the back - he had done a proper job on Blackwell's other leg!

'Oh dear.'

'Anyway, don't I know you? Your voice sounds familiar.'

'Na, we've never met before in our lives, mate.'

Dave offloaded Blackwell back at his bedside. Andi beckoned him over.

'Dave, I think you might be right, about him; look at what I've found.'

She opened Blackwell's notes, showing Dave the old typed hospital notes from years ago. The name on the top of the early notes read "Leslie Blackwell", not "Leslie Greenwell". Then she held her phone up, showing Dave the website that she had found with Blackwell and all of his previous convictions in and around the area. 'It's the same date of birth on this one I found. I'll be handing this over to social services, he probably shouldn't even be on this ward with vulnerable people! He's probably evading someone as we speak, just by changing his name.'

'No way! The dirty animal! Them notes need a flag on them, not for him to be put on here or anywhere near the kids' ward! A lady's just complained in x-ray about him staring at her little boy and saying bad stuff.'

'Will you do an incident report, Dave?'

He nodded.

'I'm going to have a word with the site manager. He needs to be put out of the way of other people.'

Dave winked at her and headed off the ward. Then he doubled back to the x-ray department to ask the clerk if the mum of the little boy had complained.

'Excuse me love, you remember that last bloke I fetched? The rude horrible one?'

'I most certainly do…'

'Well, it's just that the nurse has asked me to fill in an incident report, a little boy's mum said he was staring at him and saying stuff. Did she mention anything to you?'

'He's disgusting! I'm writing it up as we speak!'

'Great love, I was gonna write one myself, but I wasn't sure I had enough to go on. But now I know you are, that's brilliant.'

'Don't you worry, I'll put it all down.'

This was brilliant! Now Dave didn't need to write a report, and his name wouldn't be implicated should there be any repercussions. He had planted a few seeds. Sometimes, that was all that was needed. Who knew whatever else would be found out about Blackwell?

The next day, when he saw Andi, she had another story to tell him.

'Eh, you know what? It's a good job you told me about that dirty old perv changing his name! Social services have looked into him – he's got a criminal history as long as his arm! Leslie Greenwell isn't his real name! He shouldn't be anywhere near vulnerable people.'

'Really?' said Dave, trying as hard as he could to sound surprised.

'Yeah! We've had to do a safeguarding referral for when he goes home and everything to see if there are any vulnerable adults living by him. We're hoping to move him to a side room if we get one available.'

'That's disgusting that, love… when's he going home?'

'Planned for Friday morning.'

A smile spread across his face. Friday? He was down to work days on Friday. Dave would have to make sure that he was the one bleeped for the call to take Blackwell to the transport. But what if his discharge was delayed? Dave had to ensure that the depraved man would be stopped doing the things that he liked to do most ever again.

'You working Friday?'

Andi nodded.

'Well, bleep me as an emergency, just to get him out of your way.'

She smiled at him.

'That'd be great, Dave.'

Dave headed back up to the porter's office. Paul the head porter was there. He would just have to make sure that he was around, in case Blackwell was discharged earlier or later than planned. He couldn't risk not being there on the day and his plan failing.

'Paul? You still short next week?'

Paul nodded. 'I'm short every day at the moment, Dave.'

'Put me down for every day this week, mate.'

Thursday May 21st 2020

Dave needed to help Elle clear Ken's flat out. The housing association wasn't venturing into empty or unoccupied properties due to the COVID-19 threat, but according to Elle they were looking to take it back in the middle of June. As Dave was now working every day this week, he could only offer to help her in the evenings.

Dave's heart felt heavy every time he thought about Ken, which occupied most of his waking thoughts. Over the last few years, he had worried himself sick about him, now that he had gone he felt angry and resentful. Angry that Ken had never had a chance in life, angry that he had been taken away from him. But now most of all Dave felt angry with himself, angry and guilty. Guilty that he was the one that got away, that he was the one who had fallen in cow dung, and come up in life smelling of roses. Guilty that he was happy, and Ken never could be. Guilty that the recurring nightmares that he often had which involved finding Ken dead in an alleyway from an overdose, and having to identify his body had stopped. Angry because of the injustice; when had Ken ever got his justice? Now he never would, Ken was gone. Dave hoped and prayed that Ken was somewhere, watching over him. If god was real, Ken would soon see that Dave was going to make Blackwell pay: an eye for an eye and all that.

Dave looked at the picture that he had on his mantelpiece, of him, Ken and their nan. He had been nine and she had taken them to stay in the caravan in Rhyl. She did that every year - they loved it. They were all smiling, all happy! That was how Dave would remember Ken, when he was happy. When able to do so, he would take Elle on the train up to Rhyl and scatter Ken's ashes on the beach – right next to their nan's.

Ken didn't have much of any value. Dave didn't envy the housing association the task of clearing the flat. The second hand shops were shut and the price of skips had skyrocketed. Local free-cycle sites had shut down. Dave took a few pictures and cleaned a few bits and pieces to just leave outside for people to take should they wish to. Lisa was going to have a few bits of furniture for her flat to upcycle. The rest of it was getting binned.

Going through Ken's few belongings was a sad task. There was a watch that he had had since he was a kid that their nan had bought him, a couple of photographs that Dave didn't have copies of, and a little bag with some things in it. Dave opened it up and recognised the contents immediately – Nan's glasses, pill-case and her old scent bottle. Dave took them out and clutched them close to his heart. Tears began to drip down his nose to think that amongst the chaos that was Ken's life, he had managed to keep the bittersweet mementos of her with him at all times. Dave sniffed at her scent bottle; he could smell her. He revelled in the comfort for a few moments, then he wrapped them back up carefully and put them aside to keep.

That evening he started bagging some of Ken's clothes up. Most of them needed to be binned. He stayed there until late, later than he needed to stay. Then he waited until there was just enough light left. All of the other curtains in the other flats and the bungalows in the complex opposite were shut.

'Sorry, Ken, mate, but it doesn't matter now does it?'

Dave pulled on an old pair of Ken's jeans, a hooded fleece and his old boots together with some plastic gloves that he had taken from the ward with a paper mask. Just as the final rays of light in the garden began to fade away, he stepped outside into the back garden of the flats.

As spring revived, the blackberry bushes around the exit of the garden had become prominent. Soon the entrance to the sheltered accommodation would become overgrown with weeds. Dave walked through and held his breath as they ripped against the bottom of the oversized jeans that he had put on. As he gained entry into the back shared garden of Blackwell's bungalow he double-checked again - there was definitely no one around. The doors to the other bungalows were shut.

With trepidation, he turned the key in the lock and to his relief the door swung open. Dave shut it cautiously behind him. Once inside he looked around. The smell hit him - grease, mixed with stale body fluids, urine and excrement. Dave shut his eyes as it overpowered him. Flashes came flooding back into his mind, memories of bad, bad times. It was all that he could do to stop himself turning back around and walking out. But he didn't. Dave was aware that he had a limited amount of time – he could only just about see in what was left of the daylight. Not wanting to put a light on or a torch and attract attention to himself, he needed to make haste.

The place was a mess. Takeaway cartons littered the table and floor. Papers and overflowing ashtrays were strewn across the remaining surfaces. The carpet looked as if it hadn't been hoovered for months. The stench of the long forgotten full bin bag in the kitchen drifted through the house and into the mix of everything else. Dave baulked, having to stop himself from vomiting.

In the front room by the TV were piles of DVDs and video tapes. Dave shook his head - who still had a video player? CDs, films, and photo albums littered the shelves of the front room, seeming to be the only things in the house that had any order to them. There were no pictures in the house, no pictures of family, no pictures of people, nothing personal adorning the walls. These were the surroundings of someone who was very much alone - alone through choice.

Dave opened a drawer under the coffee table. In it, there were pictures. Dave nearly vomited once again as he looked. Children! Some clearly superimposed into compromising, perverted positions. Others looked genuine. Tears began to fill Dave's eyes as he forced himself to search through the drawer. He blinked them back, not wanting to leave any traces of anything anywhere, and shut the drawers now that he had what he needed.

There was little else in the bungalow. The bathroom was equally as putrid and bare as the rest of the house. He walked into the bedroom. The smell seemed to be worse in there. A wardrobe with some clothes in it that were not even fit to go to the charity shop, a bed with a duvet and pillow cases that looked as if they should have been changed a few months ago and an empty dressing table. There was a box under the bed. Dare he? Dave opened it. In there were different items. Boys y-fronts, old belts, more photos of boys. Dave didn't touch anything.

From the front window in between the blinds Dave could just about make out a children's playground; he felt even more nauseated at the prospect of Leslie Blackwell watching children, playing in a park.

Dave wanted and needed to get out of there. Knowing that he shouldn't even be in there, and reminding himself that if he messed up, or got caught, he would undoubtedly get into serious trouble and potentially lose his job, he scanned the back yard. He just had one thing left to do.

As he emerged cautiously into the fresh spring air, Dave inhaled a large sigh of relief. He had seen what he needed to see, and had done what he needed to do. It wasn't just Blackwell that he was after – there was Evans as well. But now, he needed the next part of his plan to fall into place.

Saturday May 23rd 2020

'Bleep for you,' said Ajay. 'They want you specifically, they said; maybe you got a fan club down there with the nurses?' He laughed.

Dave's heart began to race… this was it. He shook his head

'No, not with my Audrey, never, mate. Well, I wonder what they want?'

'Hello? Dave the porter here?' he said, picking the phone up.

'Dave, is that you? It's Andi. The ambulance is coming in a bit for that perv. Can you do us all a favour and come down and get him out of here to the waiting area? None of us can stand looking at him any longer!'

A smile spread across Dave's face.

'Of course I can, my love, don't you worry, I'll have him out of your ward as soon as you can say Jack Robinson!'

Dave didn't know how long he would be. There was something that he had to do before Leslie Blackwell left the hospital. His heart beat faster as he made his way down to the ward. He couldn't mess this up – it was his one and only chance. He felt around in his pocket again, and again, and again just to make sure! And there it was! As he got to the ward, Dave put his PPE on and walked in with a wheelchair.

'Dave? Am I glad to see you! He's all packed and ready to go. His stuff's in the locker by the bed, we just want him out of here!'

Dave nodded his head.

'No problem, love! Let's get him moved, shall we?'

'He's been risk assessed. They say that because he hasn't done anything for a few years and he's got no new convictions, he's not currently a threat, apparently!' Andi rolled her eyes. 'Plus he's refused carers so I'm sure he'll be back at some point, god help us, cos he'll never cope at home on his own! God knows why – he's more than happy for us all to do everything for him here!'

Dave shook his head.

'Maybe he's got something he's trying to hide?'

'It wouldn't surprise me, Dave! He's dodgy as.'

His plan had worked! The nurses had got onto Leslie Blackwell's case, they had dug a bit deeper! At least now there was a patient warning on his notes. And it was clear to everyone that he couldn't cope at home and that he needed help. None of the staff could quite understand why he had declined all offers of help, especially when he had been so lazy and demanding on the ward. Dave knew exactly why this was - the last thing that Leslie Blackwell wanted was for anyone to go to his bungalow and snoop around, open his drawers, or his box under his bed, find things, things that he shouldn't have, but that he couldn't help having, or looking at, again, and again, and again. All the personal mementos that he had of his time in power, power over people like Dave, and Ken, and all the other boys that no one cared about. All those vile and depraved pictures! Dave shuddered.

'Don't you worry! I'll get him gone.' Dave walked towards Blackwell's bed. 'Eh? Where's he gone?'

'The side room over there. We couldn't have him mixing with vulnerable people.'

He wheeled the chair over to the side room.

'Off home today, fella, is it?' he said as he opened the door and closed it behind him. Dave needed to shut the door, he couldn't let anyone or the ward cameras pick up what he was about to do.

'Yeah.'

Dave helped him into the wheelchair. Then he went to his locker at the side of the bed to make sure that it was empty – it was. Oh dear! How clumsy of him! He must have dropped something while he did it!

He gathered the rest of Blackwell's belongings together, making sure that he slipped the key back into where he would find it. Just as he was about to leave he turned the wheelchair around to face the door. Just before he pulled them open, Dave pulled out the plastic bag that he had in his pocket, and threw the remainder of the contents onto the pillow, making sure that what was left was positioned prominently.

He grinned to himself from behind his mask as he wheeled Blackwell towards the waiting area, like a proud father wheeling his new-born child out of the maternity ward for the first time. Inside, his heart raced at a hundred miles per hour as he wheeled Blackwell down the corridors and into the waiting area to be collected by the ambulance soon to be waiting outside.

Blackwell appeared to be in an even fouler mood than usual and Dave didn't make conversation. He had already chanced his luck in interacting with him, and gleaning the information from him that he had. He couldn't risk him becoming suspicious now.

Before long, the ambulance crew came to take over from him. Dave wheeled Blackwell in and shut the door. He was driven off back home to his bungalow, in the middle of the estate, right outside the children's park where all his paraphernalia was. Dave didn't bother to bid him goodbye as he would any other patient. He watched the ambulance drive off down the road. Sweat poured off his forehead as he stood wondering if his plan had worked.

Dave wheeled the wheelchair back into the hospital and disinfected it. As he walked through the ward, the nurses were gathered around the nursing station looking shocked and shaking their heads.

'Alright?'

'No,' replied Andi. 'We just found, well, some things in that pervert's locker, and his bed! We've just phoned the police.' She pointed at two books on the counter. Dave went to pick them up to have a look.

'No, don't, I wouldn't if I were you, they're sick! Deb's just found one when she was changing his bed! And he's left one in his locker!'

Dave immediately put them back down again.

'Urgh, what are they?'

'Photo albums, full of the most depraved, disgusting pictures of children!'

'You're joking?'

The staff all shook their heads, looking shocked.

Dave felt terrible. They shouldn't have had to see that. But there had been no other way of doing it.

'Sounds awful. And I've just waved the perv off!'

'It was, I feel sick!' said Andi.

'Filthy pig, how could he? Kids? What a sick perv!'

'He'll already be home by now, the police are coming down here to pick it up and take statements. I just hope he doesn't realise he's left them here and try to hide all his stuff at home!'

Dave looked at the photo albums on the top of the counter and shook his head. They were the smallest albums that Leslie Blackwell had in that drawer. Small enough for him to fetch into hospital, small enough for no one to see them in Dave's hand as he slipped one into the bed covered in a plastic bag so that his fingerprints could not be found. Dave had only had the misfortune of looking at the first couple of pictures in them – that had been more than enough for him! Just then his bleep went off.

'Well, I've got to go, girls; are you all going to be OK though? Seriously?'

They nodded.

'Yeah, just can't wait for the police to get here.'

As Dave walked off to answer his bleep, he grinned to himself from behind his mask – it had all gone to plan. He would look forward to seeing the outcome!

Sunday May 24th 2020

The next day after work, Dave went to help Elle move the last of Ken's larger items that they were taking out of the flat. Elle waited inside and Dave went in and pushed and pulled them to the door. Once outside Elle helped him to carry them down the stairs at the front for people to pick up. Apart from being helpful, Dave had an ulterior motive for wanting to be at the flat. As he walked in, Elle was just coming out in her mask.

'Hi, Uncle Dave. There are only a few bits left. The washing machine I'm taking to Mum's, the bed – someone's picking that up later, the mattress has gone, and the bloke downstairs wants the table and chairs. That's about it then. I've got a few boxes to just leave outside for people to take, and we're done.'

Dave looked at her over the top of her mask. She had the same piercing green eyes as Dave and Ken. She really was lovely; Dave felt proud of how she had turned out.

'Sorted, love, I'll just have a final look before I help you move stuff. You know, just to say goodbye.'

Dave walked into Ken's flat for the final time. He looked around, it was nearly empty. Even though this was the last place that Ken had lived in before he had passed away, it was as though he had never ever lived there. In the same vicinity as one of the people who instead of helping him, had ruined his life. How ironic that it was that fact that had helped Dave to seize his chance for retribution. He looked outside at Blackwell's bungalow; the blinds and curtains were shut tight just as he had left them.

'God, I won't miss this place! It's grim. And I dunno what's been happening out there yesterday in one of the bungalows, but the police were there all day! Fetching bags out, and stuff. It looked like they were raiding it for something!'

Elle could not see behind Dave's mask that a large smile had spread straight across his face! His plan had worked.

'Ken, you must be so proud of me, brother, wherever you are!' he whispered. 'I've had him good and proper this time, mate!'

Monday 1st June 2020

Due to the COVID-19 restrictions, there were only twenty mourners allowed at Ken's funeral. It was a beautiful service on a bright sunny day. The reverend spoke of Ken's early life, and how happy they had been living with their nan with whom he had now been reunited.

As social gatherings were banned under the restrictions, afterwards Elle and her mum Karen joined Dave, Audrey and the girls in their garden for an informal socially-distanced wake. They sat having a barbeque and drinking wine and beer until the sun went down. Even though there had been such discord and discontent between Ken and Karen, Dave and Audrey had always maintained a relationship with her. She was OK; she had brought Elle up as best as she could on her own. There was a warm and peaceful air about the evening. Despite the fact that he was gutted about losing his brother, Dave felt more at peace than he had for years. And soon, if everything went to plan, there would be retribution. Hopefully, Blackwell wouldn't be living anywhere near vulnerable people again.

Ken had wanted to be cremated, and then for his ashes to be scattered on the beach where he and Dave had enjoyed their holidays as children with their nan in the caravan. Although he had lived all over the place, anywhere his chaotic lifestyle had taken him, Ken had never been back to that beach since those happy days. It was the place where he had been happiest.

Elle wasn't sure where he wanted his ashes scattered, but Dave knew exactly where they needed to go. Deaths in the UK were continuing to rise and North Wales was now receiving the ripple from the big cities.

There was no sign, nearly six weeks into Lockdown that anything was returning to normal anytime soon. In fact, things seemed to be getting worse, not better.

Monday 8th June 2020

Dave whistled as he walked up the corridor towards A&E. Even though he was working nights this week and he was still in the middle of a pandemic, life was good. In fact, life was brilliant! Despite the fact that his brother had died, ever since he had rumbled Blackwell and his plan had worked, Dave had felt as if he was walking on air, as if someone had lifted a huge weight off his shoulders. Dave was desperate to know what had happened to Blackwell. Where he had gone? Had he been arrested? Had he been let out? Elle had handed in the keys for Ken's old flat back now and Dave was no longer able to keep surveillance on his bungalow.

He strode through A&E carrying the bag of blood that had been requested for a patient in the resuscitation department. As he walked through the x-ray department, he clocked two prison officers sitting waiting with a prisoner. Prisoners in the hospital, especially in A&E, stuck out like sore thumbs, flanked as they were by two officers dressed in PPE and handcuffed. Should they be staying in, one of the officers had to stay with them at all times. The prisoner got into a wheelchair and Ajay – dressed in the PPE worn for query COVID positive patients - began to push him along the corridor. It was Leslie Blackwell!

Palpitations began to rise in Dave's chest! So Blackwell was in prison! Whatever had been found in his flat must have been severely incriminating! Furthermore, he was unwell and being treated as query COVID positive! This was brilliant! From underneath his mask, a large grin spread straight across Dave's face. He dropped the blood off, signed the paperwork and hurried back towards the x-ray department where Ajay and the remaining guard were just leaving with Blackwell.

As he caught up to them, Blackwell sat in the wheelchair with his head bowed low, looking extremely unwell. He looked like a man who had lost the will to live, a man who had been beaten by the world. Draped in PPE, his mouth was covered with an oxygen mask and cylinder as he struggled for breath.

'You OK, mate?' Dave said to Ajay.

'Not bad.'

'You don't need a toilet break or anything? You don't want me to take over?'

'To be honest, I'm dying for the loo. I haven't been able to go for hours, I'm bursting!' said Ajay.'

Perfect.

'Er, I could do with the loo too,' said the remaining prison guard. 'I'm not really supposed to leave him though, not even to go for a slash.'

Even better!

'Jeez, you've got to go sometime! You might as well go now. Look at him, he ain't going anywhere! He's greyer than slate! I'll wait here with him, don't worry!' said Dave 'give me one second to get some proper PPE.'

'Would you mind, mate? If he goes missing, it's more than me job's worth!'

'No, no, of course not! You're gonna have to go to the loo at some point once he's on the ward anyway, ain't you? Leave him with me, I'll wait here.'

Dave dashed back into A&E to grab the more suitable protective equipment that was used for patients who were potential COVID positives. As he came back out pulling it on, Ajay and the guard headed towards the toilets. Dave waited in the corridor with Blackwell. It was early evening. There were still no visitors allowed in the hospital at the moment. All was quiet – just Dave and Blackwell: just like old times! As Ajay and the prison guard disappeared off into the toilet, Dave perused the corridor again to make sure that they were alone. He bent down.

'Back in, are you?' he said loudly, ensuring that Blackwell could hear him over his valve mask.

Blackwell held his hands out and nodded, as if to say, "well what does it look like". Even though he was ill, he still managed to be a sarcastic horrible excuse for a man.

'Did you manage to get your photos back?'

Blackwell paused, staring up at Dave. His eyes narrowed as he tried to get his breath.

'Dunno what you're talking about… what… photos?'

'Aw, what a shame. The ones they found on your bed? And in your locker? The last time you were in? You know, the sick ones of the kids? Don't suppose you've had much chance to take anymore now, have you?'

Unremorseful and unrepentant, Leslie Blackwell shook his head. 'I'm telling you! I've been set... up... Didn't even... have them on me! I'm telling you! Some sneaky bastard's set me up!' he panted.

'Yeah! Yeah, they have! Oh, you've been set up alright!'

'Eh?' Blackwell gasped as he began to pant, clasping the oxygen mask tighter over his mouth.

'I believe you, I think you're innocent. I don't think you did do it this time, did you? Leslie Greenwell?'

Blackwell shook his head.

'Na, it... weren't me!'

'Or should I say... Leslie Blackwell?'

Blackwell's eyes widened at the rim of the oxygen mask as he sucked hard, requiring more oxygen to support his palpitating heart than he was obtaining from the cylinder. Dave put his hand on the knob supplying the oxygen pressure and turned it right down.

'How, how do you know... what my... name is?'

'Oh, because we've met before, haven't we?' Dave lowered his mask. 'A long time ago now. But me see, I didn't want to be in your pictures that you've got in the drawer in your flat. You'd remember me, you and that perv, Reginald Evans? You remember me and my brother Ken?'

Becoming agitated, Blackwell stared hard at Dave.

'Who? Who are you? Don't... play... games... with me!'

'Aw, you could be a bit more friendly, couldn't you? You see, Les, we're old friends, you and I, do you remember me now?' Dave pulled his mask down further to reveal his face for a few seconds.

'It's me, Dave! Dave Williams.'

'You! You… broke my leg!'

'Ahh, you remember me now? Me and an axe, we got acquainted with your leg in the home.'

Blackwell's eyes widened in fear as he sucked hard on his oxygen despite the fact that it was no longer being pumped through the mask.

'And my brother. Ken? Remember him? Well, we didn't really like your home, specially Ken. You know your other leg? Your good leg, when it made friends with a metal bar in the park? Well, that was for him. That was me, too!'

'Y… you?'

'Me! I know where you live! I've seen your special drawer under the bed, and I found your pictures.'

'You… set… me… up? How?'

'You'll never know, will you?'

Dave pulled his mask back over his face. Blackwell's face dropped. He clasped the oxygen mask tighter, his face becoming a lighter shade of grey as he gasped for breath, not realising that he wasn't getting any oxygen.

'You? You did it!'

Dave began to laugh. Softly at first, and then louder, and louder, and louder.

'And you're right, you did leave the photos at home, in your house, didn't you? With your little collection? Of little boy's underpants and belts? And the stuff you took off the others? Off lads who had no one to look out for them? Who nobody cared about? Didn't you?'

Blackwell looked shocked, as if the devil himself had crawled up from the pits of hell and tapped him on the shoulder, as if he had just met a ghost from the past – he had, and his name was David Williams! Just some lad who had no family, nobody to look out for him, who he thought that he could do whatever he liked to. Easy prey! Or so he thought… he clutched his mask as he fought for breath.

'The ones no one would ever come looking for? Or so you thought...'

'But... how... did... you?'

'Oh mate, you're not getting any oxygen there; do you want me to turn it back on?' said Dave. 'I'd better had, they're coming back now...'

Unable to speak by now, Blackwell nodded his head vigorously.

'What was that? What did you call me?'

'P... p... please.'

'I think that the word is "sir".'

'P... pl... please... sir.'

'How do you think I got in your house to take the photos? And now you're in jail, and you've caught COVID! You're going to die...' Dave almost sang the last few sentences.

Blackwell gasped for breath as Dave switched the oxygen cylinder back on. Blackwell's eyes widened and he sucked vigorously at the oxygen cylinder.

'And I'm going to keep going till you die, until your miserable life is over! I'm going to keep causing you pain, and grief, and misery, and suffering! Just like you did to my brother...'

'N... n... no. P... p... please...'

'And when I'm done with you, I'm going to pay your old mate Reg a visit! In fact, I'm looking forwards to your stay here! I really can't wait! Think of all the fun we'll have! All the fun with me as your porter!'

'You... did... my... legs!'

'Yeah, that was me. Just like you said that night, "how much?" I don't want your money, Les, I just want to see you die... slowly... painfully...'

The toilet door opened and the prison officer and Ajay emerged.

'Has he been OK?'

'Yeah, fine. He's a bit rude though, aren't you, Mr. Greenwell? He's just told me that he thinks I'm trying to kill him!'

'Yeah,' replied the prison officer as he walked back over. 'He's renowned for being a bit rude, aren't you, Leslie?'

Blackwell's eyes were wide open, terrified. Through his oxygen mask, he was trying to say something, but failing.

'What's that, Leslie?'

'Anyway, Ajay, I'll take him up, you go and have a brew; you deserve one.'

'Oh, Dave, you're spoiling me tonight.'

Leslie Blackwell was still trying to indicate something.

Dave grinned to himself. Blackwell was in a bad way. No one would want to talk to him, to engage in any kind of aerosol generating procedure with him, that was for sure. And Dave seriously doubted that there would be a spare ventilator for someone with a bad chest and his co-morbidities. If he told people what Dave had just told him, who would believe him? Except for Reginald Evans, and how would he speak to him now? Dave would make sure that Blackwell was well dead before Evans got the opportunity to speak to him again. Now he was back in, he had plenty of time to make another plan.

As they walked off up the corridor, Blackwell began to slump forwards, clutching his chest.

'Leslie? Leslie?' shouted the prison guard, shaking Leslie's shoulders.

'Is he OK?' asked Dave, trying as hard as he could to sound concerned.

'I think he's arresting! It looks like he's got chest pain!'

Hearing the commotion, Ajay ran back down the corridor to assist. Oh no, this was not going to go to plan. Ajay had to stay as far away from his as possible!

'It's OK, we'll lie him on the ground, just in case we have to resuscitate him!' said Dave.

As Dave and the prison guard pulled Blackwell onto the floor, he looked up at Dave and grabbed out at him, trying to say something.

'You what? What's the matter, mate? Tell me what's wrong, pal…'

Blackwell carried on, pointing at Dave, trying to push him away from him.

'Just calm down, mate.'

Blackwell pulled the oxygen mask off with his final strength.

'You!'

'Can you understand what he's saying?' asked Dave.

'No, just calm down, Leslie! You're gonna make it worse.'

Suddenly, Blackwell's body went rigid, his pupils enlarged and he stopped breathing.

'He's arrested!' said Ajay.

Dave and the prison guard laid Blackwell out flat on the floor. Dave remembered what he had been taught about the latest update on resuscitating possible COVID patients.

'Ajay, he's query COVID, don't get involved, not with your asthma, just go and get some help, get us some kit and we'll get going on him'.

Eventually, Ajay returned with a nurse and crash trolley from the ward opposite. Everyone else pulled on their kits which were supposed to be COVID-proof. Dave went through the motions, doing the CPR that he had been shown in his induction. Dave was buzzing! Glowing inside, happy, only wishing that Ken was here to see this.

People flew down the corridor from all directions. They put a crash screen around Blackwell and carried on trying. Then someone took over from Dave.

After twenty minutes or so, they decided to stop, realising that the attempt to bring Leslie Blackwell back to life was futile. The CPR was terminated and the crowd dispersed from around Blackwell's lifeless body.

Dave laughed to himself as he made his way up the corridor. Softly at first, and then harder and harder and harder as he recalled the final look on Leslie Blackwell's face just before he arrested. He, Dave Williams, with no significant next-of-kin, the worthless kid from the home who had ruined his leg had managed to destroy him. The final expression of ultimate terror on Blackwell's face as the realisation had dawned was one that Dave would cherish forever.

Tuesday 18th August 2020

The travel restrictions had been lifted. Dave and Elle had something that they needed to do; to go to the beach to scatter Ken's ashes. They took the train from town and changed for the coast line. It was a bright, sunny day. The train was busy, with everyone wearing masks and attempting to keep at least two metres apart from each other.

Dave loved this train ride. Soon they could see the estuary and the sea, with the big ship docked, until eventually they got to the seaside resort where the beach was.

As they walked along the seafront, Dave reminisced about going to the caravan with their nan.

'She sounds amazing; I'd have loved to have met her,' said Elle.

'She was amazing. I don't like remembering a lot of my childhood, only the years that we lived with her; they were perfect. She's the only real part that I think about, how lovely she was, what she did for us. All the happy times we had with her, coz the rest of it was miserable.'

'I know how much Dad loved her.'

'Yeah, she was a legend was Nan. I shudder every time I think about what our life would have been like if it hadn't been for her.'

Since Blackwell had died, Dave found it easier to talk about the past. Elle was quiet as they continued to walk along the seafront. Eventually she spoke.

'I never really used to understand when I was little, you know, Uncle Dave, why you were like you were, and Dad was like he was.'

Dave sighed. 'The thing is, Elle, your dad had it tougher than me. He was that bit older. He saw more than I did, he found our mum dead on the floor after our dad had killed her. I was asleep, missed it all.'

'H… he never said…' said Elle.

'Na, it was all too painful. Then Nan died, then he got sent to the home for longer than me, which was awful, and he just ended up getting in with the wrong crowd, doing the wrong things to forget.'

As they strolled along the seafront, Dave told Elle all about the short time that he had spent in the home and what life had been like in care. She listened intently as he even told her about the axe.

'Wow, Uncle Dave. What happened after that?'

'To me? Nothing. I was just an unwanted kid from Manchester, none of them came looking for me. They didn't want anyone prying around that place.'

'My god! You could write a book about everything, Uncle Dave!'

'Na, love. I can't really write that well.'

'It doesn't matter.'

'None of it matters anymore, I've had my revenge. One day I'll tell you all about it. The thing is, I'm the luckiest bloke going. I've got Audrey, and Lisa and Emma, and Stacy, and you. I feel like a millionaire. I've got the family I never had.'

'And you'd do anything for any of them, and for me. Thanks, Uncle Dave, for looking out for me all these years. It means a lot.'

'It was a pleasure, Elle. But stop it now, you're making me a bit tearful! I'm welling up. Specially because we're now standing exactly where it was that we scattered Nan's ashes.'

They stood on the beach, thinking about Ken and Nan.

'Hello, Nan darlin', I miss and love you, lady. See our Ken here? He's comin' back to join you.' He turned to Elle. 'This is the exact spot where your dad wanted to be left when he went, right next to her. Sod this social distancing stuff, come here.'

Elle snuggled into him and he hugged her tightly. She smiled as she pulled the top off the urn. The day was sunny, and calm; there wasn't a cloud in the sky.

'Goodbye, Dad, I love you.'

Elle tipped the urn and began to shake the ashes. A gentle gust of wind crept around both of them, taking Ken's remains all around the beach, scattering them wide, back to his happy place in the golden sands.

'There you go, brother! You're back amongst it! Back in your happy place with Nan. I'll be seeing you sometime. Rest in peace! Love you, man!'

They stood for a few moments, watching the ashes dance around on the sand as Ken settled peacefully next to his nan. The sea was calm. The breeze was the only one they had felt that day and it had come from nowhere. They both knew that it was Ken; neither of them said anything, they just smiled at each other knowingly.

Tuesday September 1st 2020

As lockdown eased, things in the hospital seemed to be returning to a strange kind of normal. The number of COVID cases had decreased, visits to the mortuary were becoming fewer and more and more staff were returning to work after shielding. Gradually, the hospital was opening back up for business. Outpatient clinics were re-opening and routine operations and procedures were being reinstated. There were even drunk people and patients with sporting injuries starting to re-appear in A&E. There was a sense of hope and calm throughout the hospital that things were returning to somewhere near normal.

Dave's bleep went off. It was A&E. He picked the phone up and dialled for instructions.

'Porter.'

'I've got a patient for urgent transfer to the orthopaedic ward here.'

'No problem, I'll be down straight away.'

On the ward, the nurse in charge told him that an elderly gentleman needed to go to orthopaedics.

'It looks like his arm has gone gangrenous.'

'Ooh, nasty!'

'Yeah, looks like he's going to have to have it off. Some psycho attacked him in the park with a machete a few months ago; he's had problems with it ever since'.

'Oh dear me!'

'Although he's got two guards with him in there, so obviously come from prison. Dunno what he's done, he looks well over seventy to me! Must have been bad!'

Dave pulled opened the curtain from around cubicle. A withered-looking old man with one arm wrapped in a bandage was flanked by two prison guards.

'Alright, mate? Shall we get you to the ward?'

'One of us will be coming too,' said one of the officers. In other words, this meant that the patient was at high risk of sexual offending, extreme antisocial behaviour, a danger to himself or other people, or a mixture of all three.

'This is Mr. Reginald Evans, date of birth ninth of April 1946, going to orthopaedics please, Dave,' said the Nurse.

Dave nodded at the prison guard. From behind his mask, a large smile spread across his face. In amongst the filth and disgust in Leslie Blackwell's bungalow, there had been several useful pieces of information. Mainly the names and addresses of others. It hadn't taken him long to find the one that he was really interested in or to work out where the man lived. Luckily for Dave, it wasn't too far away. Evans always had the option of the short cut through the park, with all the vulnerable people hanging around in there! Dave just knew that it was too big a temptation for him to resist! This time, it had not been a spur of the moment thing, it had been planned.

Dave grinned to himself as he looked at the remains of Evans's arm, wrapped in a bandage drenched in green slough. Ken would be proud! He had done another fantastic job!

Dave really did have the best job in the world! How he was going to love being Reginald Evans' porter!

Printed in Great Britain
by Amazon